BLOOD RELATIONS

CAROLINE FRECHETTE

BLOOD RELATIONS

A FAMILY BY CHOICE NOVEL

Renaissance

Cover art by Franck Formantin. Design by Natasha Brousseau.

Legal deposit, Library and Archives Canada, October 2013.

ISBN 978-0-9920420-0-4

1. Winters, Alex (fictitious character) - Fiction. 2. Superpowers - Fiction. 3. Mafia - Fiction. 4. Vampires - Fiction. I. Title.

Renaissance Press

http://renaissancebookpress.com

info@renaissancebookpress.com

To Phil, who taught me to always question what I
was doing, and who saw this project when it was
just a shapeless mass of ideas.

AUGUST 23RD, 2:17 AM

The bastards always call me in the middle of the night. I haven't had a good night's sleep for over two years, if I ever really did. I tell myself, like every other night, that I'm going to set my phone to silent before I go back to sleep, but I know that at this time, no matter what it's about, the conversation is going to piss me off too much for me to remember to do it. I answer anyway.

"Yeah?"

"Alex? It's Mark. I got a problem."

"Make it fast or you'll have a bigger one."

I have to sit up in bed and put my feet on the ground to stay awake. This is business; it probably can't wait. Mark is one of my highest ranking soldiers.

"We have a big problem with Bogdan."

"Yeah, so?"

Mark might be high up, but it sure isn't because of his smarts. I find my cigarettes on the nightstand, pull one out and put it in my mouth and start looking for my lighter.

"So, he's not making payments, and he didn't show up for his appointment. He's not at his house, and now I'm showing up at the club, and there's no one there."

"And?"

"And, I think he's turning on you, man."

"That's it?" I jerk my head to look at the glaring red digits on the radio clock. "You wake me in the middle of the night to tell me that you don't have him? That nothing is happening at the moment?"

Idiot. Of course, I should have expected it. I don't need to find my lighter anymore; I know I'm angry enough to make the fire. I snap my fingers, and the flame appears between them. I manage to make it small enough not to burn the bed, this time. The smoke fills my lungs and cools me off just a little. He senses my anger; he doesn't answer.

"Don't call me in the middle of the night for shit I can handle in the morning. Now do your fucking job and find Bogdan, and call me when you have him."

I hang up before he has a chance to babble like an ass, and I smoke, thinking, maybe if I calm down a little I'll be able to go back to sleep, though there seems to be little chance of that anymore. There's too much light, and I notice that the door to my room is opening. I reach for the gun in my nightstand drawer as I turn around, but it's only Lori. I let go of the gun and stand as she walks in. She doesn't seem to be wearing anything more than a tank top and underwear, and I stare; the backlighting silhouettes the curve of her breast through the white cloth as she leans on the doorframe.

"What's going on?"

"Nothing. Go back to bed."

I rub my face. She walks closer, and the spell is broken. I can see the track marks on the inside of her arms, and it's like a cold shower.

"You can't sleep?"

"I'm fine. Go back to your room. What are you doing here, anyway?"

I walk past her and out the door. I have to get to a common area, or she'll corner me again. She turns to follow me.

"I heard you talking. Is everything all right?"

This makes me mad again, and I go back to get my smokes. I have to dodge her one more time. She couldn't have just heard me talk. I'm the only one that has a room on this floor, specifically because I get stupid phone calls from jackasses at all hours of the night. She must have been staking out my room again. Stalking me. I wonder why she's so fixated on me. There's tons of guys who don't mind her drug habit and who'd like her just fine.

"It's way too late. You know this place has a curfew."

"You're still up."

I glare at her, as I bring another cigarette to my lips. I find the anger in me and make the fire again, holding it in my hand for a long time so she can see it before bringing it up to light my smoke with.

"I own the fucking place. Doesn't mean you don't have to follow Luke's rules."

She doesn't follow me when I walk down the hall. People know better than to mess with me when I'm in that kind of a mood. I see light coming from under the door to Luke's office, so I knock and let myself in without waiting for an answer. He looks up at me over his glasses. I know he's only a couple of years older than me, probably not even twenty yet, but he still looks and acts like an old man.

"Alex. Can't sleep?"

"Stupid phone call. Lori's in my room again. Can you make her leave?"

He smiles at me in a way I'm not sure I like, and looks down at his papers again. He's always working with papers at night. He sleeps even less than I do.

"You need me to throw a girl out of your room?"

"I don't need you. You're in charge of this place, and you're in charge of these kids, and if you don't make them respect your rules, I can find someone who will."

He shakes his head like I've just told some kind of endearing joke. I know I don't have to worry about disrespect from him, but he won't let himself be bullied, either, and I like that about him. It's why I wanted him to be in charge of this place.

"I'd like to see you try. No one is crazy enough to put up with the work load. Besides, you should give her a break. She likes you; she's just not sure how to go about it. You know what she's been through."

"Hmm."

I know, and he knows I know. It's what we've all been through. I guess none of us react the same way, and I know that Lori got some of the worst of it, but that doesn't mean I want to talk about it. I concentrate to extinguish the fire from the butt of the cigarette before I toss it in the wastebasket and roll over to go to sleep on Luke's couch. He doesn't say anything, of course, he just keeps on working. I've done this a hundred times before. I like his couch better than my room, even though I wish he'd redecorate. It still looks way too much like it did when Mikov ran the brothel.

AUGUST 23RD, 10:32 AM

When I wake up in the morning, I see by the tasteless golden clock that it's past ten. Luke is gone, maybe to sleep or who knows what he does when everyone else sleeps, but the light is still on over his desk. I know he left it on for me, so I turn it off, because it's bright outside and I'm the one paying the power bill now.

I hurry back to my room to find three missed alerts on my phone. None of them are from Mark, though I missed two calls from Mister Lupino. And no wonder, either, I was supposed to meet him an hour ago. I find a clean suit as I speed-dial his cell phone, and there is no ring before I hear his light Italian accent.

"You have reached the voice mail of Domenic Lupino. Please leave me a detailed message and I will get back to you as soon as possible."

He must be meeting someone. I clear my throat to leave him a message that doesn't sound like every cigarette I smoked for the past week.

"Hello, Mister Lupino, it's Alex. I'm sorry I missed our meeting this morning, but I needed to take care of urgent business. I'll call you again later to reschedule."

Fuck that sounds stupid. I hit the red phone button and throw my cell on the bed. It bounces and crashes on the floor, but it doesn't matter. I've smashed three phones this year already. I can afford new ones.

The mini-bar that Luke converted into a game room is pretty occupied. It's raining outside, so a lot of the kids are playing foosball and pool. I think about saying hi before leaving, but then I notice that Lori's there, she's seen me, and she's coming towards me, so I skip out.

I check the house to make sure I'm not followed. I see Lori lingering through the door, and I hurry away. I know she won't follow me, she knows better than to get involved in my business; all the kids do.

The house is one of the nicest and biggest in the neighborhood. It's in the heart of the Russian district, which is where all my business takes place. It works for me because I don't know how to drive, which is the only reason I hang on to the house. I know most of the kids would like to be somewhere else, anyway.

I try Mark's cell. It's off too, and he doesn't have voice mail. He's probably asleep; most of my guys stay up all night and sleep during the day. I hang up and call Jimmy. I get voice mail, but the phone rings, so I know he'll have heard it.

"Don't leave me a message if you know what's good for you."

"Jimmy. It's Alex. I'm going to Bogdan's club and I need a ride. Call me back. Now."

I hang up. I know I'll have to call again, but with some luck, he'll check the caller ID and call me before I have to. It's just one or two miles to the club, so I start walking.

The parking lot is deserted, and I think I can see cardboard in the windows. This looks wrong; I know that this is a strip club, but it's usually open 24/7. When I get to the door, though, there's a piece of paper taped to it with the word 'closed' scribbled in black marker on it. I knock, hard enough to be heard.

"Anyone in there? Alex Winters here!"

There's no answer. The glass doors have been covered in newspapers from the inside, and I can't see. I yell.

"Hey! Open up!"

They might not be in there. But if they are, I can't let them think I'll just back off. I think about what to do, and my phone rings. I look at the caller ID before I answer.

"Jimmy! Good timing. You up?"

"I am now. Why you call me so early? You got any idea what time it is?"

"It's almost noon. Get up and get your ass over here."

"Where is 'here'?"

"Bogdan's club. They closed it up. I'm checking it out. Come pick me up."

He grumbles, but he doesn't say no outright, and I hang up so he doesn't have the time to think about it. He'll be there, even though it might take him a while. I put my phone in my pocket and turn my attention back to the building. I can't just leave. If they are trying to dodge me, I have a huge problem. It wouldn't be the first time, either. Ever since I took over the Borodinski group, almost two years ago, the smaller groups that have fallen under my control have been unpredictable, to say the least. Half the guys that swore to follow me have double-crossed me in some way, either by leaving town, trying to go independent or striking a deal with the Irish that control Old Town or the Chinese across the bridge. I thought Bogdan was solid business, since he also owned half the strip joints and pimps of the Russian district. He had seemed the least likely to jump ship, since his business depends on territory, but it seems like I was wrong there too.

The door is made of glass, and the parking lot is deserted. Should I break a window? It's quicker than trying to pick a lock, but noisier. Jimmy is better at this than I am, but I have no idea how long he's going to be, and I'm not going to be sitting in a deserted parking lot for half an hour with who knows how many Russians watching me from the comfort of their hideout.

I go around the back to the fire exit door. The back of the building faces a shipyard, so there are a lot less chances of being seen. I pick the lock like Jimmy showed me. I'm not really used to it, and it takes me a long time; when I break into places, it's usually because I want the people inside to notice. After a while, though, I get the door open, and I walk in. The place is dark, and it smells like shit, puke, and rotting meat. I haven't taken three steps in before I gotta cover my nose with my sleeve to keep myself from bringing up last night's dinner. I search the wall for a light switch through my sleeve, and my fingers feel something wet through the cloth. When I turn on the light, I can see that it's sticky, and red-brown. There's a girl down the hall in front of me. I hurry to her, but I know it's too late already.

She's sprawled on her back, her skin is too white, and her eyes are wide open. There's blood covering her neck and chest. I crouch next to her. Her neck is all mangled, like something wild attacked her. This wasn't made by any weapon I recognize. I reach for the gun tucked in the back of my pants, retrieve it, and take the safety off. What's going on here?

The bar itself is also empty, though, obviously, there was a struggle here. Some tables are overturned, the bottles behind the bar are broken, and the ground and stage are covered in glass, liquor, and blood. I survey the area carefully before stepping in, gun at the ready. There's no one around I can see. I can barely see anything, in fact, because quite a few lights have been blown out, and the place is pretty dim. Movement catches my eye on the stage, and I point the gun. I lower it when I recognize the girl, though. She's a dancer here. I think her name is Sultana, or Sveltana, or something like that. She's walking out of the back stage area, slowly. She's still wearing her stage outfit, which is to say a pink-sequent bikini, but she's got blood on the lower side of her face, and down her throat. Is she smiling?

"What happened here?"

She's definitely smiling now. She starts swaying from side to side, like she's going to start dancing, like that, covered in blood, with bare feet over the shards of glass. She speaks dreamily, with the trace of a Russian accent I remember from the only time I ever talked to her.

"Little Alex Winters is here. Poor little Alex. What is he doing here? Does he suspect anything?"

She comes towards me, swaying her hips, running her hands down her body in a way that is supposed to be sexy, smearing the blood from her throat, and chest, and on the sides of her stomach. It's not smooth; I can see that it leaves ridges between the places her fingers touched, so it has to have been there at least a little while. She rubs it over her breasts and leans towards me. I want to puke, and at the same time, I can't take my eyes off of her. She brings her hands up to grab her breasts, leaving two bloody handprints there when she moves to put them on my face. Her hands are still bloody, and I recoil from her before she can touch me.

"What the hell is wrong with you? What's going on? What happened?"

She smiles again. Her teeth look weird, like they're sharper than they should be. That's when I hear it. There are people moving about behind me. I turn around, raising the gun again. There are six of them, dressed mostly in black, surrounding me. I don't know where they came from, I never heard them come. I find Bogdan in the middle, arms folded, grinning at me with the same too-sharp teeth that the girl has. His eyes are wrong. They're much paler than I remember them being. I thought they were brown. They almost look white.

"The big man himself shows up. I hadn't expected you so soon, Mr. Winters."

I point my gun at him. He's never showed me that much respect before. Something's really wrong here.

"What the fuck is going on here, Bogdan?"

He keeps right on grinning, and comes even closer. He steps under one of the few unbroken neon lights and I see that his eyes are definitely not normal; they look almost like they're glowing. His teeth aren't just sharp; they're long, too.

"We've... gone through a little change. But don't worry; you will, too."

The psycho makes as if he's going to lunge at me, so I shoot him. I aim for the shoulder, and I can see by the change of his movements that I got him. He stops, touches his shoulder. There's blood there, if only a little; it feels like there should be more. He moves his arm like he's testing it. It should be feeling like hell now. Why isn't he screaming? I know this should hurt; I've been shot before. But he doesn't just not scream; he raises his head towards me, and the crazy fuck starts to laugh. The others laugh too. Why don't they have their guns out? They must have heard about what I can do. Why aren't they scared?

Bogdan steps towards me, hissing like a cat, his lips curled back to show his long, sharp teeth. Nothing human has teeth like that. I shoot him once more, and then another time. He just keeps coming. The back of my foot hits something, and I almost fall on the stage. I hadn't even noticed I was backing up, but by the time I've realized it, arms are grabbing me, and I remember Svetlana, or whatever her name is, was standing behind me. I try to shake out of her grasp, but she's strong, way stronger than anyone has the right to be, especially a girl that barely weighs a hundred pounds. She lifts me right off the floor at arm's length and pulls me up on stage next to her. Bogdan leaps at me like some kind of wild cat, and I'm squeezed between them. The bitch tears through the sleeve of my arm and bites me, of all things. It hurts, not as bad as a gunshot, but worse than a punch. There's no way to even lift my arm a little to shoot the gun at either of them. They're way too strong; I can't move, and there are five more out there, watching. There's only one thing I can do.

I close my eyes, and it only takes a second for me to find the hate and the rage I need to fuel my power. I make the fear go away. Who cares if they're not normal? Neither am I. I concentrate on the anger I feel toward them. About playing me. Making me break in here when they were inside. Trying to kill me. No one tries to kill me.

I don't control the fire yet, at least not well, but when I find the rage, I know how to make it, as sure as I know how to breathe, talk, and walk. I let the fire wrap around my body, radiate from every part of my being, engulf me in flame completely. I know it won't hurt me; it's MY fire. Bogdan screams and gets up, and the girl lets go. I scramble to my feet. My clothes are smoking and ruined, and the Russians are circling me, glaring at me with a lot more suspicion than before. Now they're scared. Good. I might still get out of this alive.

I take half a second to evaluate the situation. I'm on the right side of the stage, next to the main entrance and the glass doors that have been covered in newspapers. The back door I came through is unlocked, but there are four guys and a much longer distance between me and there. My firing arm is throbbing and useless, and I have to hold the gun in my left hand. I hold on to the rage, thinking about all the betrayals and double-crosses I've had to live through since I took over the Russians' operation, and I lift my good arm. I don't use the gun, though. I push the fire out of my hand and it unfurls in a wave toward the men between me and the front door. They scream and back away, and when I see that my path is clear, I run.

I'm almost at the door when one of them grabs me by the ankle. I always go down fighting, though, and I kick him in the face as I fall. Unfortunately, he looks like he barely feels it, and he doesn't let go. Since I didn't see where I was falling, my head hits the door with enough force to break the glass, tearing a whole sheet of newspaper off with it. I grab for the hole in the glass to hold on to as I feel the guy try to pull me back in, but suddenly he lets go and screams, like an animal. I turn to see. He's covering his face, backing away from the light. Is he... smoking? It doesn't matter. If they don't like the light, I can use that. I use the newspaper to get up to my feet, tearing it from the door. The light pools all around me, and these weird fucks back away from it, covering their faces and hissing. I kick enough of the broken glass out of the door to make a hole big enough to let me through, and I jump outside.

I stagger away, gun still in hand, staring at the club. It doesn't look like anything is wrong from out here, except for the newspaper and the broken glass door. Maybe I'm just having a nightmare. Are these... things what I think they are?

"What the shit happened to you, man?"

I jump and turn my gun on Jimmy. He's smoking a cigarette, leaning on the hood of his car, arms crossed. He doesn't react when I pull a gun on him, just raises an eyebrow. I realize I'm out in the open, and I quickly put the safety back on and tuck the gun away in my pants.

"Jimmy." I take a second to catch my breath. "Hadn't seen you. Get me out of here."

He shrugs, and gets in on the driver's side of the old green Corolla he's driving today. I stare at the club before I follow, but I don't want anyone to place me here, so I shake my head and sit down in the passenger's side. Jimmy starts the car and pulls away, giving me one of his neutral looks that people think are so scary.

"So, where to, boss?"

"Take me back to the house."

I lean forward to sigh, and blood rolls into my left eye. I wipe it off, and find my hand is covered in blood. Looking at my sleeve, I see it's mostly burnt and stained already, so I use it to blot the blood from my forehead, examining myself in the side mirror.

My elastic came off in the fight, but I didn't notice. Now my hair is wild, and the left side of it is completely matted with blood. There's tiny cuts all over that side of my face, too, and my clothes are burnt all over. I look down at my right arm, and see that the inside of the elbow is all mangled, and bleeding all over my lap, onto the leather of Jimmy's car. No wonder I'm dizzy. I sigh and pull out a cigarette, patting my pockets with my left hand to find a lighter. I don't find one, of course, and I don't have enough left in me to light it with my power. Jimmy just reaches in his coat pocket and tosses me his Zippo lighter. He smirks at me when I light the cigarette awkwardly with my left hand. The ugly scar that goes down the right side of his face makes his smile twisted and sardonic, even when he doesn't mean it to be.

"You should probably try to stop that bleeding."

"Yeah, sorry about your car, man."

"It's not the car."

He holds out his hand to get his lighter back. I hand it over. I don't know why he's so attached to that stupid Zippo. I know it was his old man's; but I also know his old man was a bastard who made his life miserable. He picks it up and pockets it, over his heart. He glances at my arm before putting his eyes back on the road.

"You're bleeding out. You're gonna pass out any time now. And I love you like a brother, but I ain't playing nursemaid to nobody. Gimme a smoke."

I throw my pack in his lap and I undo my belt, holding the cigarette between my lips as I keep smoking. It's not something I usually do with my left hand, but I manage to pull it off. I tighten it around my right upper arm, and keep the wound higher than my shoulder. That should get me as far as the house.

Jimmy pulls over in the parking lot, and I can see a face pressed against the window of the entrance door. I take another drag on my cigarette and turn to the driver's side.

"I'm not feeling so good after all. You wanna just go and get Luke? I'll wait here."

"Yeah, whatever."

He gets out and slams the door, and I throw out the cigarette butt. I take another one from the pack, but Jimmy is gone with his lighter, and I have to wait for him to come back.

There's a knock on the window, and I wake up. I don't know if I passed out or if I fell asleep, but suddenly Luke is there, looking worried, and I barely have the time to catch myself before I fall out of the car as he opens the door.

"Holy shit, Alex! What happened to you? Come inside!"

"No. I'll ask Jimmy to take me to his place."

There are more faces pressed against the glass; I think I recognize Lucy and Kim. These kids have seen enough horrors to last them until they're little old ladies, and I'm not going to add to them. Luke is lifting my arm, looking at it.

"You're going to pass out before you get there. How much blood have you lost already? I'll go get the first aid kit."

I guess I have no choice; I trust Jimmy as much as anyone, but I realize how useless he'd be in any situation that would require him to take care of another human being. Luke, on the other hand, was born to care.

"Fine. Get me in the garage and go get the kit. But first go get them away from the windows. I don't want them to see."

He goes in through the front door. When the garage door pulls open, he's stepping out of it with Jimmy, and it's only a second later, it seems. Jimmy comes towards the car, and I think he's going to help me walk, so I get ready to prove he doesn't have to. Instead, he gets back in the driver's seat and drives the car in the garage.

All I have to do is sit sideways on the passenger seat while Luke cuts away the sleeve of my shirt to fuss over my mangled inner arm. I lean my head on the headrest, because it's getting hard to hold it up. I see Luke frowning at me over his glasses. He turns to Jimmy, and he's trying to stay cool, but I can tell he's really worried.

"Go get the orange juice in the fridge. Bring the whole pint. And ask Sarah if she has any chocolate."

I sit up so I can make myself heard before Jimmy walks away; I'm going to need to change out of these bloody clothes before the kids see me.

"And get me a suit!"

Luke shoots me a look of annoyance, but Jimmy doesn't even say anything before he goes, so I guess I must really look bad. It doesn't feel like it should be this bad; I've had gunshot wounds that were truly terrible. This is just a little bite and a few little cuts. I didn't lose enough blood to feel this light-headed. At least, I didn't see enough blood to explain it. I think again about the way she bit me. The way Bogdan moved. Their eyes looked so wrong... I'm sure I haven't seen enough movies in my life to make my imagination run wild. Could they really be what I think they are?

"Your cell phone is ringing."

I hear it as soon as Luke mentions it. It's Lupino's ring tone, so I shove Luke aside to grab the phone out of my pocket.

"Hello?"

Luke picks up where he left off, and I let him. So long as he doesn't distract me, I don't care.

"Alex? We missed you this morning."

Shit. The meeting. I meant to call him again, and then things got... complicated.

"I know, Mister Lupino, I'm sorry."

"Is everything all right?"

"Oh, yeah, you don't have to worry, everything's under control."

"That is what I like to hear. Can I expect a visit sometime this afternoon?"

"Of course! When are you available?"

There is a sudden sting in my arm and I have to suck in my breath not to shout in pain and surprise. I glare down at Luke, but he's not paying any attention; he's squinting down at my arm, and he keeps sewing it up with black thread.

"Are you sure everything is all right?"

Great. He heard me.

"Everything's fine. This afternoon?"

There is a pause. Lupino's weird with me; he says he worries about all his guys, but sometimes I get the impression it's different with me.

"This afternoon. At two. Meet me at the park."

"I will."

"Good day, Alex."

"You too, Mister Lupino."

I glare at Luke as I hit the red button. He doesn't see me, but it still feels good.

"Couldn't you have waited 'til I got off the phone? That was Mister Lupino!"

He stops his sewing and looks at me over the top of his glasses in that old lady look he has when he's annoyed.

"I don't have to do it, you know. You can just go to a hospital."

Jerk. He knows I can't do that. I try and keep my cool.

"All I'm saying is, you could give me a warning when I'm on the phone."

"Well, what I'm saying is, you could try to avoid situations in which you get hurt like that."

"Fine! I'll quit! And you guys can just go back to what you were doing before I took over this place!"

He doesn't look back up at me, but he resumes his sewing. I think he looks hurt. I didn't mean to snap at him, but he has to understand that the job comes with the territory, and if all these kids don't want to go back to sucking cock for the Russian mob, that's just what I have to do.

Jimmy comes back with a suit in a plastic bag, a carton of orange juice and a half-eaten chocolate bar, and hands me the edibles. He opens the carton, so I just bring it to my lips. I hate the stuff. I'd rather have a good coffee, but I've come to respect Luke's medical advice. He reads a lot, and he's got all these medical books. He's better than a lot of doctors I've seen.

"There. Sorry I couldn't give you any anesthetics, but I don't have any."

I shrug.

"Whatever. It's cool."

I have a pretty high pain threshold; this is nothing compared to the shit the man my mother made me with put me through. Besides, Luke should know; he's the same.

Luke puts away his first aid stuff as I finish the last of the OJ. It is making me feel better.

"What are you going to do now?"

I check the time on my cell phone. It's almost one. I can't show up to meet Lupino looking like this.

"Gonna take a shower at Jimmy's. Meeting Mister Lupino in a little over an hour."

He starts squinting at the cuts on my face, and I start worrying about my schedule.

"Are these going to need stitches too?"

It takes him a little while to answer, but he seems pretty sure of himself when he does.

"Shouldn't. Just be careful when you wash it. If it starts bleeding again, try applying some pressure, and if it doesn't stop, call me. You should stop at the pharmacy and get some butterfly closures."

I get my feet back inside the car. They feel way too heavy.

"All right. Jimmy, take me back to your place. I gotta go have a shower."

He gets back in the driver's seat, sighing.

"Yeah, I heard."

I can see Luke's worry in his eyes as we pull away, but I just haven't got time to be reassuring anyone right now.

AUGUST 23RD, 1:56 PM

I hate being late. I'm not really late, I know, but I'm not early either, and I hate being tight when I'm meeting Lupino, especially if I have to look like some leftover side of beef from the butcher's shop.

It took a hell of a lot of shampoo to get all the blood out of my hair, and it made two of the cuts in my scalp bleed again, so I had to stop that bleeding, and then wash more blood out of my hair. I don't think I ever took a shower this long. At least, Jimmy's apartment has a lot of hot water. Luke tells me I should cut off my hair, but I won't do it. It was always my mom's job, and since I left over two years ago, I haven't been able to let someone else do it. Anyway, it doesn't look so bad in a ponytail, which is the way I usually wear it, and I don't care if Jimmy calls me princess.

The suit Jimmy picked isn't bad, at least, light gray with a dark blue shirt and tie. I check myself in the side mirror before I get out of the car. In a way, it's good Lupino wanted to meet so soon; my face has barely had time to swell, and it hasn't really started to turn purple yet, just a meaty kind of red.

I smoke a last cigarette as I head through the park with Jimmy. I won't have time to finish it, but I know Mister Lupino hates it when I smoke around him, so I smoke fast and walk slow; there's no way I'm getting through this meeting without some nicotine in me.

I throw away my cigarette when I spot Jack. He's sitting on the stone wall separating the clump of trees from the small stone terrace where the old men play chess, reading a book. Lupino is sitting at the table next to him, still in the middle of a match against a guy with a beard that seems only about forty, much too young to be there. I go stand next to Jack so he can recognize me. He looks up from his reading and nods at me with a smirk.

"You look like shit, Winters."

"At least, for me, it's an exception, which is more than I can say about you."

His grin shows his teeth, but he doesn't lift his eyes.

"Don't get smart with me, kid. You're not as hot as you think you are. Tell Blood Bath to stay where I can see him."

I glance at Jimmy. I don't know if he heard or not. He says he doesn't mind the nickname, but I do. It's not his fault he's not right in the head.

Lupino is now shaking hands with his adversary. He's won. He always wins. The man leaves, and Lupino turns his attention to me.

"Alex. Come. Sit."

He gestures to the empty seat in front of him, and I sit. He replaces the pawns in front of him. I do the same with my side. I'm not that familiar with the game yet; I have to concentrate to make sure I'm putting the right figure in the right place. He takes the white men. He always does, but only with me. I've noticed he prefers being black, but he knows I don't like to make the first move against him.

He has all his pieces placed, and the first pawn already moved by the time I'm done placing my side, and I'm already having to think before I even remember why I'm here, or what I look like. He stays quiet while I make my move. At least I can consider myself lucky that it's just pawns at this point.

He doesn't look down to see what I've done. He just smiles at me, and I suddenly remember why I've come. I pull the envelope out of my pocket. The money in it is singed, but I was able to change the envelope at Jimmy's place, so it doesn't look so bad. I pass it to him on the table, discreetly. He takes it from me just as inconspicuously, and pockets it while finally looking down at the board. His first knight comes out, and he looks back up. I don't know if he's trying to intimidate me; he knows I start having a hard time when the pieces that have names come out.

"What happened to you?"

I look up, just putting another one of my pawns out on the field to get rid of having to decide what to do. It's bad enough I have to think of how to lie to a man I swore I'd always be honest with. I have no choice, though. I'm certainly not going to tell him I think one of my biggest earners was turned into a vampire and attacked me when I went to his club.

"Well... it's just a small trouble. I'm taking care of it."

He takes my first pawn with his knight. I didn't even think to cover it. I hate the stupid way they move, in an L, like that makes any sense.

"It seems rather more like a large trouble."

I rack my brains to try and come up with both a reassuring explanation and an intelligent next move. He hates it when I don't make an effort, but how am I supposed to think when I'm being subjected to this? I see that I cleared a space for my bishop, and I move it out onto the field. I like bishops. They're decisive. They only go the one way, but it's sideways, sneaky-like, and it's hard to see them come.

"It's not. It just took me by surprise. I've got the situation under control."

He moves another pawn, threatening my bishop. I wonder if he knew what I was going to do, or if he's just so good that he doesn't even need to think about it before he makes his move. I try to match him, and I move my knight so that it'll protect my bishop's current position.

"Good, good. Just remember that I like to be informed of everything that happens when it happens. And I am the only judge of what I need to know or not."

He takes my bishop, though he knows he'll lose his pawn. I guess I should have seen it coming. I get revenge by taking his pawn with my knight, and I see him smile to himself; the wrinkles around his eyes smile with him, showing years of good humor. I guess I did something stupid again.

"You don't have to worry about that kind of stuff from me, Mister Lupino."

He moves another pawn, and takes my knight with it. Why didn't I see that coming, either? I must really be preoccupied.

"I think you are right. Still, I would hate to be disappointed in you."

We play without speaking for a few more turns. His moves seem random, unrelated to mine, but once in a while it all suddenly makes sense, always too late for me to save my men. I lose three more pawns, one rook, and another knight, and I only manage to take one of his pawns and a bishop with me. I try to look at his eyes to make sure he believes me. I can't decide. It's important he does. Not just for work, though that counts for enough. Our business relationship is complicated; when I took over the Russian operation and managed to get all of their smaller groups under me, the other large groups started testing the strength of my new organization. Lupino made me an offer then that was very hard to refuse. I don't have an official position within the family, though I am part of it. I was never made, but I report directly to Lupino, because the organization I added to his own was almost as large, if a little shaky.

Jimmy's walking around the park, looking at the trees and the wall and walking too close to Jack, trying to get a rise out of him. It doesn't work, of course; Jack is too much of a professional to get taken in by that.

"Check."

I look back at the board. His remaining bishop is putting my king in a difficult position. His queen and rook are positioned so that I have no choice but to move in a certain direction. There are no other men I can put in the way. I move.

"I understand next Tuesday is your birthday."

It takes me aback, and I have to think about it. My birthday is a vague concept, and the date is something I remember as clearly as most people remember their car's serial number. It does seem about right, though. Mister Lupino would know; he's got my permanent record. Birthdays aren't something my mom did.

"I guess."

He moves his other rook in a position that seems random, so I know he's planning something, and he's got the next three moves figured. I frown at the board, trying to push down the images of cakes and wrapped presents and parties that my friends shared with me, when I was in school, ages ago. I pick up my king to move it, but when I look up at him, I see he's shaking his head, one of his eyes closed and his lips pressed together in an expression I recognize well. I let go of the king, still watching him, and he raises his eyebrows, signaling towards my queen with his eyes. I scratch my head for a second, but then I see it. I move my queen across the board, taking the offending rook.

He has a nod and a proud little smile. I don't know what he's proud of. He's the one that taught me to play, sure enough, but I've never beat him, even when he helps me out like this. He moves his knight to threaten my queen.

"And you will be turning sixteen?"

I look at Jimmy and Jack instinctively, but I think they know how young I really am. Still, it's not something I like advertised. Lupino knows full well what age I'll be, probably even better than I do. Why does he have to say it out loud?

"...that's right."

"Do you have plans?"

Should I have plans? I don't really know how these things are done. I suppose I should talk about it with Luke.

"...not as such."

His eyes smile at me again, and they glance down at the board. I remember that it's my move, and all I can see right now is that my queen is in danger, so I move it out of harm's way.

"Good. Good. You will come have dinner at my home, yes?"

I hope I don't look too dumb when I catch myself blinking at him. I've not been often to his home, since I first broke in there almost two years ago to accept his offer, and only in official functions when there were a lot of other guys there. It's all right, though. My confusion seems to amuse him.

"Uh, yeah. I mean, yes, of course, it'll be my pleasure."

He keeps smiling as he nods once, and moves his queen to corner my king.

"Excellent. I am looking forward to it. Checkmate."

I look down and see that he's right. There's nowhere left for my king to go, and the few men I have remaining on the board are all powerless against the attack. I reach over and tip my king, and Lupino offers me his hand. I take it, careful to shake it just hard enough not to hurt him. He's getting old, after all.

"Good game, Alex. Your concentration seems to be improving."

He starts replacing the men on the board. He takes the black ones, so I know our chat is done for the day. I place the white men in front of me, and I stand.

"Take care of yourself, my boy. And I will expect to be kept apprised of your situation."

"Of course. Good bye, Mister Lupino."

He nods, smiling with the wrinkles around his eyes again. Jack pretends not to notice me leaving, until I'm right next to him. He doesn't look up when he talks to me, either.

"You might be invited, but your little friend Blood Bath stays out. That clear?"

I say nothing as I walk away. I'm going to do as he says, because it's also what Lupino would want, but I can at least let him wonder about it. Jimmy heard, this time, and he takes a second to give Jack his toothy, twisted smile before following me. He knows his reputation, and he takes advantage of it whenever he can; young guys like us, it's all we got, our reputation. Mine is for being able to do weird things with fire; Jimmy, well, he's known for being one of the scariest, craziest bastards in this city. It's completely justified, of course, on both counts. When he helped me take down the Borodinski group, he did things with his bare hands that most guys couldn't bring themselves to do with a knife. But the kind of shit his dad put him through, and after him, the Russians he was sold to, that can make a guy crazy. I think Jimmy's ok, considering.

"I didn't know it was your birthday, man."

I look at him. Him, too? I'd have thought it would have been the same as me.

"Well, I kinda forgot, myself."

"We should have a party."

Stupid parties. I concentrate on my frustration, and manage to light my cigarette with my fire. But if the guys want a party, they should have a party. They work better when they're relaxed.

"Fine, have a party. Just don't forget I already agreed to go eat with Mister Lupino."

"Don't worry. That old fart'll be in bed by the time it starts. Besides, we don't have to do it the same day."

I stop and grab his shoulder with my left hand. I give him my meanest look; Jimmy Blood Bath doesn't scare me.

"You don't talk about Mister Lupino that way. Got it?"

He rolls his eyes and reaches in my pocket for the pack of cigarettes.

"Yeah, sure, whatever."

He shakes his shoulder out of my grip. I let him, and follow him back to his car, grabbing my pack before he puts it in his pocket. He turns to look at me after he starts the car.

"So, you finally gonna tell me what happened at Bogdan's?"

He takes his eyes off me to drive the car away from the side of the street and back towards the Russian district.

"These fucks attacked me."

"What with, glass?"

I touch the inside of my right arm; the bandage is tight under the sleeve of my jacket. Jimmy's crazy, but he's not that kind of crazy. Would he believe me? Do I even believe me?

"It was just messed up."

"Did you take them out?"

"Couldn't. They took me by surprise."

"Want me to look into it?"

It would normally be what he does, and a good idea, but I don't want to send him there alone. He might be the meanest fighter I've ever met, but he's just human.

"Maybe. It'll be delicate."

"I can do delicate."

I sigh. It could be true, but I haven't seen it yet. At the same time, I can only be as watchful as my men are.

"All right. Find out what happened to the other clubs he ran. But I want absolutely no confrontations. If he realizes you're on to him, or if you encounter any situation that gets hot in any way, I want you out of there. Without waves. I mean it."

"Don't worry. I'll be discreet."

I don't know if it's the blood loss, the dehydration, or the problem itself, but my head hurts like hell. I know Jimmy thinks that being discreet just means covering his tracks, but I hope he really doesn't get involved. I need him, more than just for the rides; he's one of the only men I have that I can trust.

AUGUST 24TH, 8:38 PM

The music downstairs is loud enough to make the lampshade on my nightstand rattle. It would drown out the TV I'm watching, but I prefer to watch it on mute, since that's the way we had to watch it when I was a kid, so it doesn't bother me. Someone tries the knob, but I locked the door, so they have to resort to knocking.

"Alex? You havin' sex in there?"

I roll my eyes. Jimmy will never ask me anything emotional or personal, really, but about certain other things, he just has no sense of shame. I get up to unlock the door, let him in, then close and lock it again.

"What are you doing cooped up in here, man? This party's for your birthday! You're the man of the hour!"

I shrug, and I go to sit down on the bed. He takes the chair. I provide the cigarettes, him, the fire, and I wait for him to tell me what he wants.

"Three of Bogdan's clubs have closed. The other four remain open, but everyone swears up and down they haven't seen him. The manager of the Venus+X even told me that Bogdan hasn't collected his weekly payment yet."

"Anybody knows anything else?"

He shakes his head, leaning back in the chair, his ankle on his knee, getting comfortable.

"They might. But you told me not to make any waves, so I couldn't use any of my more persuasive methods of digging up information."

I take the rest of my cigarette to think about what to do. I haven't had any news from Mark in two days. At first I thought he was just lazy, but now I'm thinking he's probably dead. If I send Jimmy to shake down managers to find out what else they know, he might run into Bogdan, and I might lose him, too. Where else can I send him?

"Where else can you go? I mean... without making waves, still, is there someone else who might know what's going on?"

He shrugs and motions for another cigarette with his fingers, so I throw him my pack.

"I guess I can always work something out. But why are you doing this? This entire sector is ours. We should be shaking it down, especially if these guys are making trouble. You need to show everyone you're still in charge."

"I have my reasons. Just do as I say, ok?"

His face grows really still, and he looks like he's going to throw a fit for half a second, but he just ends up shrugging.

"Whatever. You're the boss."

He's worried, I can tell, but I've earned his trust by now and he thinks I'm doing the right thing. If only I could be sure he was right.

He gets up again, tossing my pack back at me.

"You coming down?"

"I'm not a party person."

"Come on. It's your birthday. Everyone wants to see you."

He knows what to say. I follow him down the stairs. All the kids are there, even those who didn't stay to live here after they were free. There's a couple of the men that work for me, too, but very few; only the ones that kind of like me. No one that's just here to impress me, or at least I think. Good. That means that Luke and Jimmy did at least manage to keep it quiet. I stop to see a couple of the guys. Some of them owe me money, anyways. I do my handshakes, thank them for coming so they don't feel obligated to stay, pocket the envelopes some give me, and make small talk where it's required. They seem satisfied after a few minutes, and they make polite excuses to go. I can't even see Jimmy anymore. Is he gone? He's the one who wanted to throw this party.

I see Lori chatting with a couple of the girls who left. She must miss them. She's the oldest one here, now. She hasn't noticed me, so I go in the kitchen. Luke is there, pouring chips into a big orange plastic bowl. He smiles at me when I come in, looking at me over his glasses again.

"Hey, birthday boy! Want a beer?"

"Nah, get me a soda."

"You sure? You are sixteen, now, you should allow yourself to party a little."

Since when is Luke trying to encourage me to party? I see he's drinking himself.

"I'm going to be sixteen tomorrow. And I don't drink."

He frowns at me. He's looking through his glasses so he can get a better look. He's figuring out something; he's got that face. I know it's something about me, and I don't know what.

"Will you just get me a fucking soda?"

He nods, but he still has his thinking face on. He hands me a store-brand cola, my favorite kind of soda, and I pop it open, drinking a big gulp of sweet, bubbly caffeine. He takes the bag he just emptied in the bowl to throw it in the garbage, and then looks up at me, not picking up the bowl.

"Everything all right? You seem pretty preoccupied these days."

"It's fine. I just don't like wasting my time."

He smiles and shakes his head.

"Have a little fun, Alex. You're all about working and business and responsibility. Take a night off! Relax. If anyone deserves it, it's you."

"I don't like parties."

He rolls his eyes and puts his hand on my shoulder.

"Come on. I haven't seen you go to a single one since I met you, and that was nearly two years ago. It's not hard to see that your last party must have had a clown and a pin-the-tail-on-the-donkey game."

He spins me so I'm facing out of the kitchen again.

"Go have fun. Drink some beer. Talk to a girl. Live a little!"

He gives me a little encouraging push, and turns to pick up the bowl of chips. I stay there for a few seconds, sipping my soda. Most of the guys that work for me are gone, though a few have remained to hit on the dozen girls between thirteen and twenty that are still hanging around. I should go tell them to back off; the girls here are off limits, and they should know.

I haven't taken three steps when Lori comes out of nowhere, and she's suddenly standing right in front of me, smiling. There's no way I can dodge her without being awkward. She's wearing a low-cut green dress with long sleeves. It's really short, too; it looks nice on her.

"Hi, Alex."

"Oh, hi, Lori."

"Happy birthday. I got you something."

She hands me a small, flat square box wrapped in red paper. I take it, and turn it over. The paper is carefully folded, and stuck to the bottom with a single strip of transparent tape. Am I supposed to take off the tape, or rip the paper? I've never gotten a present before.

"Uh... thanks."

"Well? Open it!"

I decide to go for the delicate method, and I carefully pull the tape off the paper before unfolding it. It's a white cardboard box. I open it, push aside the blue tissue paper and retrieve a thin, silver cigarette case. It's good quality, seems well built, and I think it's actual silver. I turn it over in my hands, open it. It might hold a whole pack. I smile at her. This is real classy, just the way I like it.

"Thanks! This is really nice!"

I take out my pack to put the cigarettes inside, and look for somewhere to put down my soda. She takes it from my hand, nodding for me to follow her into the living room. I do, walking slow, transferring my cigarettes in the silver case. They fit perfectly, nice and snug, and the case fits much better in the pocket of my jacket than the packs they're sold in.

She sits on the couch, still holding my soda, and she pats the empty spot next to her. I look around; it seems we're alone, except for a guy I don't know lounging in a comfy chair near the fireplace. The furniture in here is still the same as it was when this place was a brothel. It's gaudy and golden. I should get Luke to change it. I sit next to her, putting the empty cigarette pack on the table. She hands me back my soda, and I drain half of it; for some reason, my mouth is dry. She's just smiling in that confident way she has, like she knows more than I do and she thinks it's funny. I put a cigarette in my mouth so I don't have to talk; I don't know what to say.

"So how come you didn't tell anyone it's your birthday? I had to hear it from Jimmy."

I shrug, and finish my soda.

"It's just a day. It's the same as the day before and the day after."

"It's important!"

She puts her hand on my knee, and I lean forward to put the empty can on the glass top of the golden framed coffee table to hide the fact that I'm jerking away from her.

"It's not, really. Why would it be important?"

She watches me. I can't read her expression; I suppose years spent here made her an expert at hiding how she feels. I know she's not smiling as much as she was when she gave me the present, though.

"Because you're important. To us."

I toss the butt of my cigarette in the empty can, and light another one.

"I'm just the one in charge. If it wasn't me, it would be someone else. Luke does a pretty damn good job."

"Are you kidding?"

She seems pretty intent, so I look her in the eye. She doesn't look angry, exactly, it's more like she can't believe what I'm saying. The guy sitting in the chair next to the fireplace gives us a look. I get the impression he's listening to our conversation, but I can't place him. Was he a kid here when I took over? I don't think so; first of all he doesn't look that young. He doesn't look that old, either, but I think he must be over twenty. Is he the boyfriend of one of the girls? Why isn't he with her, then? Lori's voice brings me back to the moment, and I forget about the guy for now.

"I mean, you're right, of course, Luke does a good job, but he would be dead and we would still be in the same shit we were in, if you never came here."

I pick up my can, and it rattles softly, so I remember it's empty save for the cigarette butt and I can't drink from it anymore. I guess she's probably right, though I can't possibly take the credit for helping them. I was pissed off, which is why I did what I did. I barely knew anyone else was in trouble until I had killed most of the people that were in charge of this hellhole. All I did was stay to help, afterwards, and I'm almost sure Luke would have been fine without me. It's not something I want to get into tonight, though, and not with her. So I shrug, don't answer, and hope she gets the hint.

She stays quiet until I'm done with my smoke and throw the butt out in the can. I'm suddenly feeling really tired, and my head is spinning, like when I smoke a cigarette after I haven't eaten for twelve hours. I rub my face to wake myself up, and start to get up. Lori puts a hand on my forearm to stop me.

"What do you want? I can get it for you."

"Can you get me another soda?"

"You don't want a beer?"

I shake my head. It feels stuffy, and heavy, and I think I can feel my brain bouncing loosely inside.

"Don't drink. Soda. Coke, if there's any left."

She gets up and walks back towards the kitchen. I lean against the back of the couch, resting my head and closing my eyes. I don't feel sick, exactly, just dizzy and weird, but it's not entirely unpleasant. I feel someone sit next to me again and I open my eyes, expecting to see Lori back already. Instead, it's that weird guy that was sitting next to the fireplace. What's he want with me?

"Hey."

I don't answer, just stare at him. I hope I look as pissed off as I feel right now. I don't want to be bothered. He's drinking beer, and he takes another swig before looking back at me.

"Not too talkative."

"What do you want?"

He smirks, and downs the rest of his beer.

"It's not really about what I want. But you're looking into something that's a lot more trouble than you imagine. Here."

He digs through the back pocket of his jeans, pulls out a faded, crumpled business card, and hands it to me. I squint at it, but for some reason I can't read it; the letters are all blurry and I can't make any sense of them. He gets up, and I see that Lori's back, she's standing next to us with two beers in her hands. The guy says nothing, goes away. She sits back down next to me, and puts the beer in my hands. I want to tell her that I don't drink, that I'm pissed off and that I want to go to bed, but it all seems like so much trouble, like so much effort, and I'm thirsty, so I just take a sip. Just one sip isn't going to affect me, change me, make me like him.

I feel her hand on my leg again. I want to tell her to back off, jerk away, but by the time I have enough brains to react, her face is right in front of mine, and her lips are all over mine. I try to talk, but she just puts her tongue in my mouth. I can't think, suddenly. The only thing that exists is her mouth, and my mouth, and I don't understand anything else anymore.

AUGUST 25TH, 10:08 AM

Warm. And soft. Everything feels good for a few seconds. I can smell something like my pillow, and sweat. There's a warm weight on my chest, and I feel something - no, someone - pressed against my back.

I open my eyes, the surge of adrenaline so strong that it twists my stomach, making me feel sick, and all I can think of is it's happening again, I have to get away. I scramble out of the other person's grasp and end up on the floor, my leg tangled in the sheet. That's when I realize that I'm in my own room, in no danger, and that it's just Lori in the bed. I feel like a fool, but only for a second. I realize that she's still asleep, hasn't seen me, and so my embarrassment disappears, leaving room for my anger. Doesn't she realize how lucky she is? That last time I woke up in bed with a stranger, a lot of people ended up dying? What the hell is she doing in my bed, anyway?

I stand to disentangle myself from the sheet, and I see that I'm naked. She seems to be, too. I try to think, but I can't seem to remember anything past the point where that weird guy gave me his card, and then she kissed me. Why'd she do that? What happened after? I only had one sip of beer. Didn't I? Why can't I remember anything? Did I get drunk? I seem to remember skin, and tongue, and a nice, warm feeling in my balls, but... I can't make sense of it. I mean I'm not stupid, but... I can't think of events, or anything.

I look on the nightstand and see that her kit is there, with the needle and plastic tubing out. I have a paranoid thought, and check the inside of both my arms. The left one is intact, and the right one is still tightly wrapped in bandages, same as it was yesterday. Seems like that, at least, she kept to herself.

As the adrenaline recedes, my head starts throbbing, and the nausea I thought was only 'caused by the fear just keeps getting worse. I'd go back to bed, except I don't want to wake her. This may be my room, but I just don't want to have to talk to her right now. I grab a suit quietly, make sure my shirt and tie match, pick up fresh underwear and socks, and then I sneak out to go have a shower. I don't wake her, and I don't encounter anyone else in the hall.

I take the quickest shower I know how to, then tie my hair while it's still wet, and dress in a hurry. I don't even take the time to shave; I shave every day, even though I don't really have to yet. I just think if I do it often enough, maybe the hair on my chin will finally become full, or at least evenly distributed.

Luke sees me come down the stairs, and he smiles, coming towards me. I make for the exit, pretending I haven't seen him standing five feet away from me.

"Hey, Alex! Wait up!"

I get out, pull the door shut behind me, and walk down the driveway. Luke knows better than to call out after me when I'm outside, and I manage to get away without having to make eye contact. I don't know what I did last night, and I don't want to know. At least, one of the privileges of being the boss is that if I don't want to deal with it, I don't have to.

I reach in my pocket to grab my cell phone and call Jimmy, but I realize that I don't have it. I don't have my cigarettes, either. Damn. Now I need to find a payphone.

AUGUST 25TH, 1:48 PM

I never understand how Jimmy spends his time. Sometimes, it takes him forty-five minutes to get from his place to the house, sometimes it takes him ten. Today, it takes him two hours to come and meet me at the coffee shop three blocks down from the house. He doesn't come in to get me, he just parks in front of the terrace and honks, so I leave a ten-dollar bill on the table and hop over the fence to get in on the passenger's side. He's driving an old Honda Civic. He seems in a relatively good mood when he greets me, so I don't give him shit about the time it took him. He tosses my silver cigarette case and my cell phone in my lap, giving me a sly smile.

"Here you go, boss. I never figured you for one to bang and run. Anyway, if you were gonna do that, you might have chosen some girl who doesn't live with you."

"Shut up. I didn't call you here for that."

He seems amused, but he doesn't say anything more. He's learned not to push me when I feel like this.

I open the cigarette case to retrieve a couple of smokes for me and Jimmy, and I see the crumpled white business card that weird guy gave me last night. There's no name, no address, no company, just a single phone number printed on it. Who was that guy?

"So, where to, boss?"

"Bogdan's club."

Jimmy takes his eyes off the road to raise his eyebrows at me. I can tell he's surprised, but he's also pleased.

"Changed your mind?"

"Yeah. You're right; I can't let these assholes fuck with us."

The truth is, I'm pissed off right now, and I feel cornered, which represents the best possible set of conditions for me to use my fire, and I've had enough of jerking Jimmy around and keeping things from him. Besides, I don't want to feel crazy and uncertain anymore. I need someone else to see it, too.

We park in the empty parking lot. Everything seems the same, at first glance, except the glass door I broke was boarded up.

Jimmy starts to get out of the car, but then he notices that I'm not moving, and he settles back inside, looking at me. I hand him a cigarette, looking at the club, wondering how I'm supposed to do this. I can't let him go in there blind.

"Problem, boss?"

He lights his cigarette. He's acting casual, but I can feel him tense up anyway, like a spring waiting to be released.

"Well... maybe. There's something you should know about these guys before we go in there."

"Sure. What is it?"

"Well... they're not... normal."

He smokes his cigarette, watching me sideways with that careful neutral expression he has when he's approaching a situation he's not sure about. He doesn't answer, so I go on.

"When I shot them, it didn't hurt them. And they were afraid of the sunlight."

He waits for the rest, and it takes me a while to work up the courage to say it.

"Man, I think they're vampires."

He doesn't answer right away, just turns to watch the club, his jaw tight, the scar on his right cheek puffing with the effort of his containing himself.

"I don't like it when people fuck with me, Alex."

"I'm not fucking with you! Have I ever fucked with you even once since I met you? You know I don't mess around with the job."

He turns back to me, examining me carefully. The scar makes the serious expression on his face even more intense; his right eye seems to be glaring at me from beneath the odd angle of his eyelid. He knows I'm right; I'm not exactly the joking type. After a long moment that could be five minutes or half an hour of tense, heavy silence, he finally replies.

"All right. Vampires. Shit. If it had been anybody else than you, man..."

He shakes his head. I know what he means. I'm probably the only person in the world he actually trusts, if he really even does that, and on top of that I can make fire out of thin air. In a way, I guess it's lucky it happened to me. I would have never believed one of my guys coming up with that story.

"So, got a plan?"

I think about it for a second.

"Well, I'm looking to blow off some steam right now, so I'm thinking about burning them. Beyond that, your guess is as good as mine."

He looks at the building and nods.

"All right. We'll improvise, like we always do. Let's go."

He grabs the baseball bat he keeps on the back seat of whatever car he happens to drive, and leads the way to the club. He gets us through the front door by picking the lock so fast I barely even see him do it. Once we're inside, I get the idea to remove all the paper from the remaining door. It doesn't hurt to have all the advantages you can get, no matter how small.

The place looks the same inside as it did before. I try to stay pissed off, but it's getting hard, 'cause I'm getting jumpy. I think I see something moving next to the stage, and I think I hear something weird, but there's nothing there. The blonde girl's body isn't where it was when I came here the day before yesterday, either. The way to the back door seems clear, and entirely free of dead girls.

We make it to the main room. This time, I definitely hear hissing. It's coming from the small hallway next to the stage that leads to the changing rooms, and the meeting room where Bogdan and his pals like to hang out. Or liked to, I guess. The door leading there is closed, so I jerk my chin towards it, and motion for Jimmy to break it down. He gives a good kick, and as it flies back, swinging open, he jumps and raises his baseball bat. Immediately, there's a sort of rasping, throaty howl, and a cop jumps out at Jimmy, except there's blood down the front of his uniform, and he's lunging at us with his fingers held out like claws. I get ready with my fire, but Jimmy was already waiting for him, and he swings the bat full force. The cop's momentum is halted, and he hits the side of the stage instead of landing on Jimmy.

Jimmy moves in for a second hit, but the guy gets up right away, like it was nothing, and grabs the bat in mid-swing. Jimmy tugs on it, but the vampire yanks back, and he just falls right into the monster's clutches. The cop grabs him by the throat, and goes to bite his neck, but Jimmy's not that easily done in, not even by freaky vampire super strength. He tries to push the monster away, putting a hand on its face, and he rams his thumb into its eye socket, making the eyeball burst like an overripe grape. The thing doesn't even sound human when it screams. I take advantage of the distraction to grab the vampire cop by the back of its collar and pull him off Jimmy; I manage it halfway, but the moment I feel there's enough distance between it and Jimmy, I grab its throat, and pour my rage into it, making the flames burst from inside its bones. It's easy, really. He tried to eat my friend.

The thing screams, and lets go of Jimmy. He gets away while I keep holding the thing's neck in my hands. It screams and writhes as its flesh crackles and roasts, and the thing finally explodes in ash and embers. I'm still staring at the empty air between my hands when Jimmy speaks.

"Holy shit, man. You weren't kidding."

"I told you I wasn't."

I feel mildly offended. Even for something this unbelievable, I had thought Jimmy would have taken my word for it. He looks through the door, picking up his baseball bat again.

"Should we go see if there's more down there?"

I try to wrap my head around it. Why was this one wearing a cop uniform? Where are the others? Wouldn't they have attacked us too if they were still around? They must have gone, and left this dude here as some sort of decoy or trap. It's the only explanation.

"I think they've moved on from here. They would have shown up by now."

Jimmy nods.

"Yeah. Maybe we better move on, too, before someone calls about the noise and the weird car in the parking lot."

We get back out, and I'm not too unhappy to be standing in the sun again. Jimmy heads straight for the car, and I follow him. He's right; we have to get out of here as soon as possible. He drives us back in the general direction of the house, gesturing for a cigarette. I give it to him, taking one myself, and I light us both.

"So, what are we gonna do about them vampires? Think they got out of town?"

I take a long drag from my cigarette before answering.

"Not a chance. They're around, and I don't know what they're up to. The first thing to do is to assign someone to the strip clubs and the girls, the ones that we have left. I'll put Ivanov on it, and tell him we're fighting a break-off so he understands some of the risk. I want you to scout around the clubs that have been closed, and find out in which one they're most likely hiding. And seriously, don't try to take them on alone."

"Don't worry, boss. I might be a little fucked in the head, but I ain't stupid."

I nod. This should give me ample time to find out how to hurt these bastards. It's good to know I'm not crazy, either.

AUGUST 26TH, 4:46 PM

Lupino's house is not as large as you'd expect, though it is really fancy. It's in the nice part of the Italian neighborhood, made of gray stone and dark red tiled roof. It's fenced in by a wall made of black iron and the same stone as the house. The front yard is full of plants, and there's a thick vine covering half the front of the house. The yard is big, but it looks small because of all the plants; I know the back yard is much more crowded, though.

I knock on the door, wait a little bit. Jack finally opens it. He frowns at me, like he's disappointed I showed, then looks over my shoulder to make sure I'm alone. I am, of course; Jimmy had things to do. He seems almost sorry to let me in, but he does, and closes the door. He leads me through the foyer to a small living room, the one I've never been in; we usually meet outside, because Mister Lupino doesn't like to conduct business in his home. There are a few comfy chairs there, and a low oak coffee table on which is a marble chess set. What impresses me the most is how many books are on the shelves all around. He seems to like them a lot, too; his bookcases are pretty nice, some of them have glass doors and everything.

There's a fireplace in the far wall, near the table with the chess set on it. Above the mantelpiece is an old black and white picture in a large, gilded frame. It shows a younger version of Lupino, maybe about forty or so; his hair is a lot darker, the way it used to be, though there are patches of white showing at the temples. He has his arm around a woman that looks to be the same age, early forties, and a guy that could be my age, maybe a little older; he looks like Lupino. I wonder who they are. I never heard anything about Lupino having a family.

"Hello, Alex."

I turn around. Mister Lupino's coming in. He's not wearing a suit as usual, more like a shirt and tie under a wool sweater.

"Hi, Mister Lupino."

He folds his hands over the small of his back, and walks towards me, hunching just a little. He looks up at the picture, still smiling, though his eyes squint a little. I look at the picture again, afraid to ask. I don't like it when people ask about my past, so, as a rule, I don't ask about theirs. He seems to be in a conversational mood, though.

"My wife, Sofia, and our son, Nicola."

I don't want to ask, but I don't want to be rude, either; it's the sort of statement that demands follow-through, or at least I think.

"That looks like an old picture."

He turns to smile at me. There's something about his expression that reminds me of Luke when he's figuring out something about someone. He looks at me for a while, then looks back at the picture. His smile is faltering; there's memory in his eyes, and pain.

"Yes. They passed away shortly before I left Italy to come to America, some thirty years ago."

He pats my shoulder gently, as if in complicity.

"It is a great burden to be responsible for someone else's well-being. Come, now. Dinner will be served soon."

I follow him out the door of the living room and into the dining room. He walks slowly, so I fall in next to him not to be impolite.

"How goes your problem with your man Bogdan?"

I didn't tell him it had to do with Bogdan; I guess he really does know everything everyone that works for him does.

"Actually, we had an interesting development yesterday, and the situation is returning under my control. It should all be sorted out before the end of the week."

He smiles without looking at me. I think he looks proud. Maybe it's just in my head.

"Good. Good."

The table in the dining room is oak, and looks old; there are no pictures on these walls, just a window behind the head of the table, and a small crystal chandelier over the center. He sits at the head, and motions for me to take the seat right around the corner, next to him. I do. Only these two places have been laid out and prepared.

"Jack isn't eating with us?"

Lupino shakes his head.

"He has gone home already."

Well, that's a mercy, at least, though it's always a little intimidating to be alone with Mister Lupino. A plump woman in her fifties comes out from a door behind me, carrying a bottle of wine and two glasses. Lupino smiles up at her, motioning to her with his hand.

"Ah. Alex, you have met Rosanna, my cook?"

I have, once or twice, but never really formally. I just nod at her, because I'm not sure what I'm supposed to do to be polite. She puts down the glasses and bottle on the table, takes out a corkscrew and grins at me. She's definitely not a looker, but there's something warm in her smile, that makes you want to curl up and listen to her sing you a song. Her accent is much thicker than Lupino's, and it makes her voice sing when she speaks.

"Alex! Yes! I have heard much about you."

She leans down to kiss both my cheeks, holding my face in her hands for much longer than is comfortable.

"Mister Domenic, he thinks very good of you."

I blink at her, and nod. I hope I don't look too stupid; I'm not used to physical affection.

"Uh, thank you."

She pats my cheek and lets go of me, but frowns at the healing cuts on the left side of my face and scalp. She squints, looking closer. It only lasts a second, after that she just looks at me, clicking her tongue in disapproval.

"You are handsome young man. Should take better care of your face."

She finally gets to opening the bottle of wine. Lupino seems to think her little display was pretty funny; either that, or my face is, right now. She starts pouring the first glass, and Lupino finally asks.

"Would you like some wine, Alex? It is a very good year."

"No, thank you. I don't drink."

Lupino seems surprised, but then he nods, as if it makes sense.

"I can respect a man that looks out for his health."

I nod, as if to agree. That's not the reason why I don't drink, of course, but I don't want to get into that with him right now, or ever, if it can be helped. He knows too much personal stuff about me for my comfort as it is. As Rosanna hands him his glass, I think there's something apologetic to his smile.

"I hope you will forgive an old man his habits."

I nod. I don't mind if he drinks. He's probably fine, and I can't imagine him losing his mind from drink, not Mister Lupino. Besides, wine's not really the kind of thing you get drunk on. Rosanna picks up the other glass.

"I can bring you homemade lemonade."

I nod. I haven't had the stuff since I was a small kid, but I remember thinking it tasted all right. I don't want to seem too fussy, anyway.

She goes away, and Mister Lupino reaches over to a small table beneath the window he has his back to, picking up a wrapped present I hadn't noticed was there. The paper is silver, and kind of shiny, and there's an elaborate ribbon and bow on it; it looks like it was wrapped professionally. It's small, though it's more than four times the size of the one Lori gave me. I wonder what it is. I've never gotten presents in my life, and now that's two in three days.

"Happy birthday, Alex."

"Thank you, Mister Lupino."

I unwrap it. It takes patience to remove all the ribbon and tape so I don't damage the paper, but it feels expensive and I don't know if it's offensive or not to rip the wrapping off. The paper is thick, much more than the one Lori's present had been wrapped in. I unfold it carefully. It's a book, bound in red leather, with the words 'Machiavelli - Il Principe' written on it in gold letters. I stare at it for a second. I don't think I've ever finished a book, not even those I had to read in school, when I still went, and I don't speak a word of Italian. I flip through it. It doesn't have illustrations, exactly, but more like really fancy lettering on certain pages. One side is in Italian, but the other seems to be in English. At least, I'll be able to read it, if I ever find the time.

"Thank you."

He smiles, and I see I haven't offended him with my awkwardness. At least, there's that.

"I know you probably do not read much. But this book is very good, and there are things in there that might help you with the decisions you make every day. Besides, it might improve your Italian."

I raise an eyebrow at him. Is he suggesting I learn Italian? He sees my expression as he brings the cup of wine to his lips, and laughs instead of taking a sip.

"Do not worry. You do not have to learn Italian. But it is one of the world's most beautiful languages, and it would add much to your culture."

I look down at one of the pages. Looks like I'm learning Italian. For some reason, it's important that Mister Lupino thinks highly of me, sometimes way beyond my professional performance.

Rosanna comes back with my lemonade. It's good, much better than I remember it being. She smiles in satisfaction when she sees my face, and goes back to fetch the dinner.

It's some kind of pasta, with chicken. It doesn't taste like anything I've had before; the only kinds of pasta I've ever eaten were frozen lasagna, and macaroni and cheese from a box. This stuff doesn't even compare, it's some of the best food I've ever eaten. Lupino smirks at me as I wolf down the first four or five bites, shoveling as much food as I can get into my mouth at one time.

"Good, is it not?"

I nod. It's like I can't control my hand, and as soon as I've swallowed, I take another bite. He chuckles, and takes a much smaller and more dignified bite than I do. He chews slowly, but his enjoyment is evident.

"Rosanna's homemade pesto is one of the finest I have tasted. When I first came to America, I spent ten long years trying to get used to hamburgers, missing the food from home, before I found Rosanna. I do not know what I would do without her."

I nod again, this time more enthusiastically. I can't seem to put my fork down; my mouth is too full to talk. He takes a few more small, slow bites, while I clear off my plate. He calls out to his cook, saying something to her in Italian. She comes, and takes away my plate. I don't dare ask for more; I probably look bad-mannered and uneducated enough as it is. At least, he's not commenting.

"Are you still living in the Mikov house?"

That came out of nowhere.

"Yeah, I am."

Rosanna comes back with my plate, and it's full again. I thank her, and she smiles warmly at me, making a weird dismissive wave with her hand. Lupino's smiling at me too. I start eating again, but more civilized-like, this time.

"Are you settled there for good, or do you plan on moving out?"

I have to think about this; it's never really come up. I stay there because the kids are there, because there was room enough and it's ours, now. I suppose I should move out eventually, though. My business isn't exactly the safest.

"I haven't really thought about it yet, Mister Lupino."

He nods.

"Of course, of course. You are a busy man."

"Why do you ask?"

"Well, I was wondering if you would consider taking one of the rooms in this house."

"Seriously?"

I stare at him, not thinking about the food anymore. It only lasts a second, though, after which I realize how stupid I have to look with my mouth open, and I clear my throat, taking another bite and chewing it slowly, if only to have an excuse not to be talking. I have no idea how to follow my stupid outburst. Fortunately, he goes on.

"I cannot say I hate the idea of having someone of your... particular talents under my roof. Though this could be to your advantage, as well. You take very good care of the children, young and old, in that house of yours, Alex. But you should have another place, one that belongs to you, where you can rest your head."

He picks up his napkin from his lap, and wipes his mouth with it before putting it down on the table. He seems to be done. I keep eating.

"I am an old man, Alex. I do not have a family anymore, not for many years now. I have grown very fond of you over the time I have known you. You remind me very much of Nicola, my son, you know. It would be good for an old man to be in the presence of youth again."

He's serious. Not only that, he seems to have thought about it for a while. I take another bite. This food is great, and I certainly wouldn't mind having that kind of food to eat three times a day, even if it ends up making me fat. I guess it's true what the guys say, and Lupino really does have a soft spot for me. I'm not sure what to say. My first impulse is to say yes, but I can't think straight right now, and I need to take time and analyze this to make sure he doesn't have an ulterior motive.

"I'll think about it, Mister Lupino."

He seems happy about my answer.

"Excellent. Rosanna made some tiramisu for your birthday. You will see, it does not have its equal this side of the ocean."

AUGUST 26TH, 11:07 PM

Jimmy starts the car as I get in and slam the door. He looks tired; I wonder if he was asleep. He glances at Lupino's house through the metal gate, and then looks at me.

"So? How was your dinner with the old man?"

"Great, actually. Really great. How was your evening?"

"Good developments. I got back four bars. There's only the Exxxotic where I didn't get to talk to anyone in charge. I say we go back in the daytime."

"You think that's our spot?"

"Could be. I got a vibe."

"All right. I gotta look into this a bit more before we can go."

He pulls into the street, starting to drive out of the nice neighborhood.

"So, boss, am I taking you back to your place this time?"

I check the time. Lori will probably be in bed, but maybe not.

"I don't know. Do you mind if I crash at your place again?"

He chuckles, shaking his head. The scar makes his smile look like a sneer.

"Are you planning to ever talk to the girl?"

I glare at him. Since when does Jimmy get involved in my personal life?

"It's none of your business."

"It is if it means you're moving in with me. I'm gonna need a bigger place. I need a lot of personal space, you know."

I suppose I am imposing on him. Jimmy doesn't invite people to his place lightly. I shouldn't take advantage of it too much.

"Fine. You win. I'll go talk to her tomorrow."

I look out the window as he drives us back to his place. Maybe Lupino has something when he says I need a place of my own.

AUGUST 27TH, 2:19 PM

The house seems deserted when I get inside. I don't explore to make sure that it is, and head straight upstairs. At any rate, chances are high that there really isn't anyone there. School has started, and we've enrolled everyone here, under fake identities, of course. It's one of Luke's rules. He says everyone has to learn to become independent and to fend for themselves, and he says that if they don't go to school they have to get a job and pitch in. I hope Lori's out job hunting. I know she refuses to go to school. I should have at least an hour and a half until they start coming back.

I make my way up to the third floor, where my room and Luke's office are. I peek into my room, which is the door closest to the top of the stairs, as I pass it. The bed's been made, there's no trace of Lori, of what happened, or that there is anything wrong. I make sure she's not hiding somewhere, and head to Luke's office.

Luke is there, lying on the couch, asleep. I guess he has to take it where he can. I'm careful not to make a sound as I make my way to the computer on his desk, and I even remember to turn off the speakers before I boot it.

I hate computers. My mom and the man she made me with never had one, and the ones at the school I went to were so obsolete that they couldn't even work email, so it's a skill I never developed. I have Luke take my emails for me when I think I need them taken, and I try never to have to use it for anything.

When the evil machine is finally done starting, it takes me nearly ten minutes to even find the Internet. When I do, it takes me to some place called Google, and I type the word vampire, press enter, and start looking through the 67 billion results that it turns up.

All I find is shit. I mean, I'm pretty sure I've seen the real deal, and these guys aren't sweet, tortured, or glittery in the sun, and since that's all I find after looking a good ten minutes, digging deeper to find better stuff is beyond both my skills and my patience. I can't ask anyone else to do it for me, 'cause they'll either think I'm crazy or going through some kind of Emo phase.

There is the sound of a cell phone alarm eventually, and Luke wakes up. He looks at me, he's obviously surprised to see me, and there's a hint of panic in his gestures as he feels on the coffee table for his glasses. I remember he can't really see me without them, so I reassure him. He's also had his share of waking up next to strangers who didn't wish him well.

"It's just me, Luke. Everything's fine, I'm just using the computer."

He relaxes, finds his glasses, and sits up, putting them on.

"Hey, Alex. It's been a while since we've seen you. I've been worried. Is everything all right?"

"Yeah, yeah, everything is fine."

He looks at me with his concerned expression. I can tell he doesn't believe me, but that's tough. I don't feel like sharing.

"Anything you want to talk about?"

"Not really. I'm busy."

He gets up and walks to stand behind me, looking at the screen. There's a Wikipedia page open about vampires that I was looking at; it's about all I can find that makes any sort of sense at all. I try to lower it before he sees it, but I'm not used to computers and I don't manage it. He squints at it, and then frowns at me like he caught me eating my boogers.

"Vampires? Can't you just look at porn like everyone else?"

I give him a look. I know that he, of all people, would never look at porn. And I, at least, wouldn't go looking for it.

"It's just... curiosity."

"Uh-huh."

He raises an eyebrow at me, and seems to think for a few seconds, then just shrugs.

"Need any help?"

I consider it. He's much smarter than I am, and he actually knows how to use a computer. Besides, he already knows what I'm researching, so the harm is done. I might as well ask.

"Yeah. I wanna know about vampires."

I get up to leave him the seat, and he sits down. He touches the mouse a couple of times, and types on a couple of keys on the keyboard, and before I can tell how he's doing it, he's lowered my Wikipedia window, and he's got another search going.

"Anything in particular?"

"Uh... like what?"

He uses that patient tone he has with people he thinks are stupid.

"Well, you know... do you want to know about vampire movies, or their place in mythology, or what?"

"I want to know how to kill them."

He blinks at me with a slight frown and his mouth open for at least five seconds, looking sort of like an angry fish, then he turns back to the computer. His fingers hover over the keyboard, but don't move. Eventually, he turns to me with an expression halfway between concern and puzzlement.

"Really? Are you sure you're all right, Alex?"

"Yeah, I'm all right, no, I'm not crazy, I just need to know this stuff. Or better yet, can you find me someone around here who knows about all that?"

"You're serious."

"Yeah, I am. Now will you help me or do I need to learn how to use this stupid thing?"

He shrugs, raising his eyebrows and shaking his head.

"All right, all right, I'll help you. Just, if you are going nuts, give me a heads up, won't you?"

"Uh... sure, whatever."

I take a cigarette from the silver case Lori gave me and glance at the weird, crumpled business card as I light it, using my fire. I wonder if I should call this guy. Who was he, anyway? What's his angle? I watch Luke go, and put the card away. Luke's real smart. He'll find something.

I leave him to it as I walk out of the office. He'll work better if I'm not around.

AUGUST 27TH, 9:57 PM

I wake up when the door opens. I don't remember when I fell asleep, but it must have been some time ago. Now, I feel weird, like I slept too much or too little. I sit up, rubbing the right side of my face, trying to look like I'm more awake than I feel. Lori comes in, and closes the door behind her. She has a smile I don't like on her face as she walks towards me, swaying her hips like I've seen the strippers do. I stand up, suddenly more awake.

"Lori. What are you doing?"

"You left! I missed you in the morning. And then, you don't show up for two days! I was worried!"

She puts a hand on my chest, and slides it up over my shoulder, stepping closer in the same motion. I see her pupils are dilated, and I recognize what I don't like in her smile; she's high, she probably shot up just before coming in here. I push her away, gently, so she doesn't fall. She pouts at me, and it makes me feel a little bad, but I still take her elbow and lead her to the door.

"I was busy. I still am, so go to bed, Lori. In your own bed."

I open the door and lead her outside. She starts protesting, and I try to retreat back in my room to avoid it but she jams her foot in the door.

"You can't just have sex with me and then not talk about it."

"Go away!"

She glares at me. Her eyes are bloodshot, and it makes her look a little scary.

"You're a bastard, Alex Winters. Just like everyone else."

I think she's going to storm off, but she folds her arms and keeps glowering at me. For some reason, I don't really want her mad at me. I just want her to not be there, or not to be high, that's all.

"I'm not a bastard. I just don't want to talk about this with you right now."

"Why not? I do! You've been missing for two days, you bastard!"

She tries to punch my chest, poorly. I grab her fist to stop her, and then push her away gently.

"Not when you're like this. If you wanna talk about it, we'll do it when you're not high, I promise."

She knows that's not negotiable. She grits her teeth, obviously still seething, but she just turns and walks away.

"This isn't over, Alex Winters!"

I lean against the wall in the hall, sighing, pulling another cigarette out of the silver case she gave me. I stare at it for a second, and try to make fire to light my cigarette, but I just can't. I start searching my pockets for a lighter. Luke just shows up out of nowhere next to me, lighting a match. I keep forgetting his office is just down the hall. He must have heard the whole thing. I let him light my cigarette without a word, and don't look at him as he shakes the flame off. He walks into my room and to the ashtray on the nightstand to dispose of the burnt match, then turns to look at me, making no move to walk back out.

I walk in slowly, and close the door. I don't really want to go further in, so I lean against it, and stare at the floor. Luke pulls the chair away from the desk and puts it close to the bed, sitting on it. Looks like he's expecting a conversation. I don't go sit, though. I'm still in control of the situation, here.

"You know you're going to have to deal with this eventually."

I give him a mean look, but it never really makes him back off. I keep smoking, but he doesn't answer, forcing me to fill the silence.

"Deal with what?"

"Well, if you did sleep with Lori, you should talk about it with her. She'll be expecting your relationship to grow into something else."

I sigh, and give in; I go sit on the bed. This is not an area of expertise for me, and maybe Luke can actually help. I try to think hard about what happened that night, but it's still a complete blank. When I look up again, I see Luke is frowning with one of his figuring-out expressions.

"Tell me what's on your mind, Alex."

"I don't know."

I try to think of what else to say, but that sentence pretty much sums up the way I feel about everything right now. He won't let it rest, though.

"What don't you know?"

I shrug, but he waits for me to talk, so I do.

"I think... I think I got drunk that night."

I throw the butt of my cigarette in the ashtray, and grab the matches to smoke another one.

"So?"

"So? So, I didn't even want to get drunk and I did anyway."

I rub my face again, and accidentally pull at one of the cuts that go into my scalp. It starts bleeding again, but only a little, not enough to make a mess.

"Alex, about this drinking thing..."

He reaches to touch my knee, but stops himself in time, changing the motion into a vague gesture to support his speech. He knows I don't like to be touched, but he's gotten used to touching the younger kids when they're sad or they need comforting.

"I don't really know how to put it. But we're not our old men. Not you, not me, not Jimmy. And even if you do drink, it doesn't mean you'll do anything bad. I mean, look at Lori. She doesn't seem hurt."

Is this supposed to make me feel better? I don't answer. I'm starting to feel pissed off again. It feels so much better than feeling sorry for myself. It's Luke's turn to be intimidated by the silence, and he keeps talking.

"How much did you drink, anyway?"

"I don't know. I only remember taking one sip from one beer."

He's quiet for too long, and I look up at him. He's making his thinking face again. I hate that I don't know what I say that makes him do that; it seems to be something different every time.

"What?"

"What do you mean, you only remember taking one sip?"

"I mean I don't remember what happened after that."

"Like, you can't count the drinks you've had?"

I shake my head. I wish I could remember at least that much.

"No. I can't remember anything past that. Like, maybe impressions. But nothing that makes sense, or that I can put together."

"Ok, give me a play-by-play."

I frown. What's he driving at? Does that mean I dodged the talk about Lori? I don't ask, in case I did.

"Of what?"

"The evening. Since I saw you in the kitchen."

"There isn't much to tell. I met with Lori, and I went with her to the living room. You should really change the furniture, by the way. Just name your price, but I hate the shit that's still there."

"Yeah, ok, I'll get one of the girls to take care of it. But what happened in the living room?"

"Nothing. I talked with her just a little. Then I started to feel funny. She got me a beer, and I took one sip from it. Oh yeah, while she was gone, this weird guy came to talk to me."

"What did he want?"

"He gave me his card."

I pull out the cigarette case, take another cigarette, and hand Luke the card.

"That's weird. Did he say who he was?"

"Not that I remember. I'm not even really sure what he wanted."

I think about it for a moment. My head was starting to go when I talked to the guy, but I have the vague memory he was trying to warn me about something. Was he trying to scare me?

Luke hands the card back to me.

"And you started feeling funny after you drank the beer?"

I shake my head.

"After I finished my soda. Why?"

He makes a face. I'm pretty sure I know what he's thinking, but I'd rather he say it first.

"What happened after the beer? What do you remember?"

"She kissed me. And after that, not much. I woke up in bed with her, and I really can't remember anything that happened."

He nods, and stands up.

"I don't think you need to worry about your drinking. And don't worry about Lori. I'll talk to her."

"Tell me, Luke."

"I think you've been roofied."

I should have known. Why didn't I know? He walks to the door.

"Don't get pissed off, ok? Let me handle this."

That's easy for him to say. Don't get pissed off. He's not the one that was tricked like that. It could only have been her. Unless it was that weird guy, but why would he do it? She did hold my drink. Both of them. Luke's giving me that worried look again.

"Seriously, Alex. I'm sure she didn't mean any harm by it."

"Are you fucking kidding me?"

I wanna punch him now; but I could never hurt Luke.

"Look, Alex... it's really complicated, relationships. After what she's been through. What we've been through."

"I know."

"Well, that's the thing, Alex, you don't know. You don't know what it's like."

The hell I don't. Who does he think he is, anyway? He's doing that thing where he reads my mind again, 'cause I don't have time to say what I want before he answers it.

"What I mean is, I know what your dad was like. My dad was pretty messed up too. But you don't know what kind of hell this place was before you came."

He shakes his head. It's not entirely true. I've seen enough to get an idea of what it was like, but he's right, I don't know.

"What she did was wrong. But I know she really likes you, and, well... I guess she's just not sure how to express it."

I don't know what to say, so I don't answer. He sighs.

"Anyway, like I said... I'll talk to her."

He starts to walk away, but I call out to him before he's out.

"Hey Luke. Keep her out of my way for a while, won't you?"

"Yeah, I don't think you'll have to worry about her anytime soon."

I light another cigarette. The case reminds me of her, and I snap it shut so I can put it away as soon as possible. He walks out without another word. I get up and go lock the door so I don't have any more unwanted company.

AUGUST 28TH, 6:48 PM

The building doesn't look like much, but I have to hope this guy knows something; he was the only person Luke could find that I could talk to. I guess the Internet is great if you're looking to have sex, but finding vampire experts is a bit more difficult.

The shop is in Old Town, so I check myself. I'm allowed to shop all over the city, I mean, I'm not doing something really official or anything, but I don't want anyone, rival or not, to see me going into a place called 'The Black Cauldron Magick Shoppe'.

There's a bell when Jimmy pulls open the door for me. The place smells like a church at a funeral, and one full of old ladies, at that. It's not like in the movies, though, with all sorts of creepy crap like skulls and rats and snakes lying around all over. Everything is in shelves, or on top of velvety red displays, and most of the stuff is wrapped in cellophane. The books all look like they've been printed this century, too. It's actually even kind of cozy, because of all the old-fashioned posters and drapes. It looks mystical, whatever that means. There's a weird bead curtain that's separating the main store from another area, though; maybe the snakes and skulls are in there.

The guy behind the counter is a short, round guy with glasses, pimples and a hairline that's started to recede already. He's got Celtic tattoos all over his forearms, and he looks almost tough when he raises his eyes from his magazine to see us. But when he does, his attitude changes, and I can see that he's panicking a little. I guess he doesn't get many customers like us. I'm a little disappointed, though. I kinda expected an old English guy with a bowtie that says things like "confound it!"

"Can I help you guys?"

I look at Jimmy. I'm suddenly doubting Luke's ability to find me what I need. He shrugs, like he's saying, why not try anyway?

"You Philip Thornton?"

He frowns. I think I can see the sweat forming on his brow. I mean, come on. We're not even trying to scare him. Well, I'm not, anyway. Jimmy's grinning, and it's hard to tell if he's trying to be friendly or terrifying.

"Uh... yeah, why?"

"You're supposed to be able to help me with a... problem I'm having."

I look around quickly. The shop seems deserted, but I signal Jimmy with a motion of my chin to go have a look. He does, keeping his eyes on Philip Thornton for a little while as he does. The shopkeeper watches him with a worried face before turning back to me.

"What... is your problem, exactly?"

"I want to know what you know about... vampires."

He stares at me. He's trying to decide what to think, I can tell.

"Um... vampires?"

I nod, annoyed. I won't repeat it. He scratches his head, taking another look at Jimmy.

"Well... what do you want to know?"

"What you know."

"Well, they sleep during the day, hunt at night..."

I click my tongue, annoyed. Is this guy a dumbass?

"Look, I was told you were the man to see about vampires. And I'm not talking about the crap that's in the movies. So either you can help me or you can't. Either way, make it quick."

"Who are you?"

"Is that relevant to your ability to help me?"

Jimmy's back with a nod. There's no one else in the shop. At least, there's that. Philip Thornton pushes his glasses higher on the bridge of his nose.

"Well, no, I guess not..."

I start drumming my fingers on his glass counter. He clears his throat and finally puts down the magazine.

"Well, why do you need to know?"

"I got beef with a couple of them."

I keep my eyes level, my face serious. It feels ridiculous, being here, and if that fucker laughs, I'll beat the crap out of him. He doesn't, though. He looks at me like he's trying to tell if I'm kidding or not. He glances at Jimmy and decides that we're serious.

"Um... so you want to know what, exactly?"

"I want to know how to kill them. And how to find them."

He walks out from behind the counter, retrieving a cardboard, handmade sign on which is written 'back in five minutes'. He goes to the door, tapes the note to it, and locks it from the inside.

"Well, you have come to the right man, and at the right time, too. Follow me."

He takes us to the back store, through the weird bead curtain. This leads to a place that fits a lot more my image of what a magic shop should look like, if only marginally. No skulls, though. There is a big table with lots of books, candles, and weird crap like feathers and eggs and glass jars and bottles. There are shelves, but these ones look old, and have a bunch of dusty old books on them. On the right side is a map of the city, with colored pushpins inserted at various places, mostly throughout the Russian district. There are a few clippings pinned on the wall next to it, too. I look at them briefly, but then look at the guy. I hate reading, and I have a feeling he's going to give me the Cliff notes, anyways. He heads to the table, where he picks up a book and starts leafing through it.

"What do you already know?"

I shrug. What do I know?

"Not much. They don't like the sunlight, they have fucked up eyes and teeth, and they don't seem too tortured about what they are."

"Yeah, it's not like the books. Sunlight will definitely more make them burst into flames than glitter. They're vulnerable to fire, too. And you can cut off their heads and put a stake through their hearts."

I've seen enough vampire movies to know that's not everything.

"What about all the other stuff? You know, garlic, crosses, holy water, all that junk?"

He makes a face and bobs his head from side to side.

"Garlic does work, though really not as well as you would think. As for holy symbols, well... there are mixed reports about that. Sometimes they work, sometimes they don't."

"Why don't they work all the time?"

He shrugs, looking at his book.

"Depends. Most people say it has to do with the faith of the wielder. But I think the willpower of the vampire also has to do with it. And his age."

"His age?"

"As I understand it, the older a vampire gets, the stronger and more resistant to harm he is."

I think for a second. Bogdan and the dancer were impossibly strong. And I've seen Bogdan in daylight, not two weeks ago. Is that guy saying that they get even stronger?

"Anything else that can help us?"

"Well, the part about them not being able to come in someone's home unless they're invited is true. That doesn't mean that they can't find a way to make you come out, like burning it down or throwing a grenade or something."

I think about it, but Jimmy jumps in with a question of his own.

"So, what, we go around poking them with sharp sticks?"

Philip closes his book, shaking his head.

"No way. Forget what you saw on TV. The heart's under the sternum, and there's no way anyone can break through bone even that thin with a single hit, especially with a wooden stick. It'd take super strength. The only way you're killing a vampire with a stake is if you've got a hammer and a way to incapacitate him."

I guess that makes sense. I've never tried it on someone else before, but the man my mom made me with broke my arm twice, and three of my ribs, and I know how much it takes to break bones. And I was tiny back then, not a two-hundred pound badass Russian vampire. Thornton goes on.

"And beheading is the same thing. The spine is an incredibly hard bone to break, and if you don't sever it completely, your vampire will be able to get better and maybe even counterstrike."

I smirk at Jimmy.

"Good thing I'm good with fire."

His face contorts into the twisted expression that serves as his smile, and I turn back to the expert.

"All right, so how do I find these fuckers?'

"You after the new group that's trying to settle here?"

Now that's unexpected. This guy is way more informed than he seems. Maybe his advice is better than I thought.

"What do you know about that?"

He glances at the wall where the news clippings are pinned, and shrugs with one of his shoulders.

"Well, I moved here because of this town's low activity. Stuff happened at my old town... anyway, this town was famous for not tolerating the formation of any new groups."

"Why not?"

"Well, I'm not sure, really. Just, vampire gangs don't seem to form here."

"Until now."

He nods reluctantly.

"Until now."

"So, where do these new guys come from?"

"I don't know. But they've only been here a couple of weeks. And they seem to be only targeting the underbelly of the city, like prostitutes and drug dealers, from what I've gathered, so it's hard to measure their advance. Most of these disappearances don't make the news."

"Do you know where they're hiding out?"

"Not the specifics. But they seem to be acting in this corner of that neighborhood, there."

I look at where he points on the map. I'm not sure what the dots are, but they do seem to be located all around the red light part of the Russian district. It fits; I guess Jimmy was right. They must be hiding out at the Exxxotic.

"So, you done a lot of vampire hunting, before?"

The guy shakes his head. I'm not sure, but I think he looks a bit ashamed.

"Not really. I just like to keep informed. I mean, I did manage to kill one, in my hometown, but I had to in order to survive. I don't know if I'd be able to do it again, and I certainly wouldn't go looking for the opportunity to try."

I look at him. He doesn't look like much, but if he says he killed one, I guess he might be saying the truth.

"How'd you do it?"

He looks down again. This time, he's blushing.

"Burned down its house in the daytime. There was really not that much to it. It was actually kind of an accident."

"Hey, whatever works, man. If you got it, you got it. How much do I owe you for the info?"

"Don't worry about it. I'm glad to help, if you can get rid of them. I liked this town when it was quiet. Just, if you get in trouble, have the kindness to keep my name and my shop out of it."

I've never known this town to be quiet, but then I've never known there to be vampires, either. I guess everyone does live in a different world. I nod to him, and let myself out.

AUGUST 29TH, 10:17 AM

The Exxxotic is located very close to downtown, on the lower East side of the Russian district. Its parking lot is accessible through an alley that goes by the side of the building. Jimmy parks on the street, about a block away, because we don't want the car to be seen coming.

It doesn't look like much from the outside, just a brick building with a few windows and a door, all of them plastered with pictures of nearly naked girls. All in all, it could be the perfect place for vampires to hide; I'm pretty sure there isn't a single window left in this building through which you could see the light of day. Jimmy takes us to the rear, careful of the sound we make going in front of the windows. I wasn't sure about bringing him, but he insisted on coming. He says he'll be fine, but from what the guy told me, even someone as scary as Jimmy Blood Bath is pretty much helpless against a real vampire. But he seems to have brought much more than just his baseball bat, this time. He's got a whole duffel bag full of goodies.

He takes a crowbar out of his duffel, and just forces the back door open. In this part of the city, we have much better chances of being seen, so speed is of the essence. I jump in first, and he follows me inside.

The back door leads to a small kitchen that seems to be mostly used as a secondary storage room for the bar. I find an empty bottle to jam the door open with, so we have a little bit of light coming in. Jimmy checks the two small storage areas on our right, and I take a quick look around the kitchen. It's deserted, but everything seems to be in order.

There's a door at the far end, which probably leads to the bar, and one to my left. I'm not sure where that one goes. I try it, and it's locked. I look at Jimmy to see what he thinks, and he gestures towards the door that leads to the bar. I go in front of him; we've agreed I should be first. He follows me, baseball bat at the ready.

This door is unlocked. I twist the knob as quietly as I can, and pull the door open slowly, looking inside before rushing in like a fool. The place looks deserted too, so I make my way inside, checking every corner. There's nothing broken behind the bar, and the chairs are all turned up on the tables, like they had a perfectly normal night followed by a perfectly normal close, yesterday. I'm starting to doubt that this is the place.

We step out from behind the bar, and Jimmy goes to check the coat room while I keep my eye on the stage. I don't think they're hiding in the coat room. If they're anywhere, they're probably in the back stage area, and the only way to there is through the curtains behind the stage or the hallway on the far side of it.

I glance at Jimmy as he gets back from the coat room. He's shaking his head; he didn't find anyone. I don't want to climb over the bar that surrounds the stage, so I decide to head for the hallway. I walk a little faster, and I'm a bit less careful about the noise we're making. I'm starting to think that we really were wrong, that this can't be the place. It's too normal, too quiet.

I don't hear anything, but I notice Jimmy stopping. He lowers the bat, his eyes on the curtain, and he reaches into his duffel bag to take out one of his pre-prepared Molotov cocktails. I stop too, following his gaze. There's a corner of the curtain that's moving slightly, just a flutter. It could be a draft, but I don't feel any wind. And I'm pretty sure it wasn't moving a moment ago.

We stare at it so intently and for so long that it doesn't look like anything anymore, and the small movement eventually stops. I look at Jimmy, but he's still frowning at the curtain, and he gestures for me to go check it out. I sigh. Looks like I'll be climbing the bar after all.

At least, I don't have any gear to put down. I put one knee over the bar and hoist myself up over it, reaching the stage in two strides. I take three steps towards the curtain, and suddenly it flies in my face. I stumble back, trying to get the cloth away, but it tangles around my arm and the next thing I know, I'm being knocked down on my back on the stage, with a face that seems to be made entirely of glowing eyes and huge, pointy teeth inches away from mine.

I manage to hold it back with my forearm against his neck; the teeth are so close I can feel how sharp they are, and a little bit of spittle drips from one onto my cheek. He's way stronger than I am; his teeth just keep getting closer and closer, until a bottle breaks over his head, and flames pour out of it, engulfing both of us. The guy screams and gets off of me, running around in circles on the stage. I stay down. It takes all my concentration to quench the flames with my mind, but I know I can do it. A good part of the front of my suit has been burnt, but I seem to be ok. Jimmy's reaching me with his jacket. He stares like he doesn't know what I can do yet, and he's about to say something, but I don't give him the time.

"Are you out of your fucking mind?"

"Well, yeah." He shrugs dismissively, and looks over at the flaming vampire as it bursts into ash and embers. "But you're fine. And he's not. So it worked." He extends a hand to help me up. As I take it, the curtain moves again. I push him back so I'm standing in front of him, and I find the anger in me so I can make enough fire to give our new friends a proper greeting. I start it as a wave, and it quickly builds up into a wall. The first two that launched themselves at us back off suddenly. One of them catches on fire, and he throws himself to the floor to roll. There are more coming behind the fire, though; I think I see as many as four that are still standing, plus the one that's managed to stomp off the flames and get back up. I maintain the fire wall to protect Jimmy, but I concentrate on how many suits this stupid business has cost me so far and I manage to make more fire come up from under them.

Two more catch fire, and they jump out of the way, rolling. I wish I could maintain the fire on them, but I can't do that and keep up the wall at same time. I'm already feeling my anger slipping, and my concentration can't hold up. I just hope Jimmy's gonna throw another one of his bottles sometime soon, and as I think it, I hear glass breaking and a vampire screaming. It's not coming from in front of me, though, so I turn around to see Jimmy lighting another one. There are four of them in front of him, too, though I can see the one he lit up burst into ash. He's holding his own, and so am I, but there are a lot more than I thought there would be. I'm tackled again and thrown to the floor. The fire vanishes from my mind, but there's still light, so I guess I managed to set something on fire.

The thing is trying to grab me, expecting a struggle, but I let it, grabbing it right back. I make the fire inside him like I did the first time, and the thing doesn't even think to bite me, he just screams and writhes and bursts. I get up and shake the embers and ash off myself, and I can see that Jimmy has managed to set two more on fire, but he's losing ground fast. I don't know if he's out of bottles, but he's swinging his baseball bat wildly to keep them away from him. There's five, now. The ones I had been keeping away with my wall of fire are surrounding him. I take a quick look around myself, but there doesn't seem to be any more coming from back stage; besides, now, the curtain is burning, and part of the stage, too. If there are more, I don't think they'll be coming from there, so I turn back to focus on Jimmy, or rather the vampire that's just managed to wrench the baseball bat away from him.

I concentrate. I'm starting to feel weak, and it's hard to keep up the anger I need; I can feel that my palms are sweaty, and my breathing isn't as easy as it was before. I still manage to make the fire, though at this distance, and without touching him, I don't manage to make it come from inside him. I do manage to keep it on him long enough for him to blow up in ashes in that fucked up way they do, and for Jimmy to get away from the two remaining ones, and closer to me.

The other two vampires seem to hesitate, looking at each other before they look at us. It's funny, I don't think I've seen Bogdan, or the dancer. I wonder if Jimmy killed them. I'm starting to feel pretty good, and confident. After all, Jimmy and I just killed five of them, and only two remain. Jimmy looks up at me with his twisted grin, but then I see his face changing, like he's seeing something behind me.

"Watch out!"

I don't have time to see what it is. Something grabs me by the arm and leg, and throws me. I fly across the entire bar, at least forty feet, and I think I hit the opposite wall, bounce off of it and crash on the floor, 'cause I register at least two painful hits on top of one another, but I'm not entirely sure what's going on anymore.

There's an explosion, and a blinding light. I see Jimmy come up from where he's hidden on the other side of the bar. That crazy fuck brought grenades, though they seem to only be flash grenades. He looks at me and screams something, but I can't hear him because of the ringing in my ears. I try to warn him about the vampires that are recovering from the explosion and coming towards him. There are three now; I guess there were more of them after all. Why is Jimmy still shouting at me? Can't he see they're coming for him?

I turn my head slightly and see what he's shouting about. There's another one, a new one, heading straight for me, with the cocksure grin of someone who knows he's won. I try to get up, and the pain suddenly coming from my shoulder and ribs almost makes me scream. I guess I have a couple broken bones.

I glare at the guy coming towards me, try to hate him for the confidence of his smile, his walk, for breaking my bones. But all I can think of is, that's it, this is the end, I'm finally going to get it this time, and the fear is much too sharp to let any anger through.

I try to fight him as the guy picks me up, but every movement hurts my ribs so much I can't breathe. I at least manage to spit in the fucker's face. He takes the time to wipe it off and smile at me, and I hate him almost enough to cut through the fear, at that moment, though something else is catching my eye. I know this guy, I'm almost sure of it. He's not one of the Russians, but I've seen his face before.

It's the last really clear thought I have, as the guy sinks his sharp teeth in my neck. Compared to the pain in my ribs and shoulder, I can barely feel this. I try to fight, but I feel the strength leaving my muscles with every passing second. This is it, then. I thought I had a few good years in me yet. I wish I had prepared for my death better; I don't know how the kids are going to do without me. I hear a loud crash, like a lot of glass is being broken at once, and then, nothing.

AUGUST 29TH, 11:12 PM

I wake up, and the first thing I feel is pain, everywhere, intense and debilitating, and I know, at least, that I'm not dead. Unless I am dead, and I've gone to hell, but I'm not sure I really believe in that crap, and if I did, I think it'd probably hurt a lot more.

"You awake?"

I don't recognize the voice. My vision is a bit blurry, and I can't see where I am, but I think I'm lying on a leather couch; I can smell it. As my eyes focus, I can see that it's brown, and that there is another couch exactly like this one in front, across a small table that I've never seen before.

I try to sit up, and the pain in my shoulder intensifies a hundredfold, which is still nothing compared to the one in my ribs. I manage not to scream, just moan a little, and I think you'd need pretty good hearing to hear it.

"Settle down, kid. Here, drink this."

Someone sits on the coffee table and hands me a glass of water. I take it automatically, and the guy leans toward me. I try to scramble away for half a second, but I hurt too much to move, and he only puts his arm under my shoulder to help me sit up. It still hurts, but less; besides, I've had a lot worse before. He puts a couple pillows under me to help support my back. They're orange and brown, with flowers on them, like they're straight out of the seventies. He sits back down on the table and grins at me, and that's when I place him.

"You're the weird guy from the party! The one with the business card!"

"That's me! Call me Erik."

"Where the fuck am I?"

My throat feels suddenly very dry, and I start coughing. Then I realize I have a glass of water in my hands and drink the whole thing without catching my breath. The guy takes the glass after I'm done, and stands up. The thought occurs to me that it might have been poisoned, or drugged, but I don't care. Besides, I was just unconscious. I suppose if he wanted to drug or poison me, he had better chances.

"Want anything else? Beer? Coffee?"

"Got any soda?"

He shrugs.

"I'll check."

He walks out of my sight, and I take advantage of his absence to take a better look around. I'm in a weird living room, full of really old furniture, way older than Lupino's. The wallpaper is the ugliest I've ever seen; it's brown and beige, with dark brown flowers printed on it.

There are thick, heavy brown curtains covering the windows, and there's no TV. I try to get up to go see under the curtains, and normally, I would be able to work through the pain, but I can't do it. I feel weak, and my head spins as soon as I try to sit up by myself.

The guy comes back, putting down a can of honest-to-goodness Coca Cola on the coffee table in front of me.

"Found it in the fridge downstairs. I have no idea how old it is, though."

I shrug. It's cold, it's still sealed, and it makes a fizzing sound when I open it. I drink a quarter of it before I catch my breath, and put it down again. The guy who calls himself Erik sits on the other leather couch.

"Ok, so where am I and what am I doing here?"

"You're in my house. I brought you here."

I try to think. The last thing I remember is being killed by a vampire. But the vampire wasn't this guy. I have a million questions, suddenly, and I'm not sure where to start. Then it hits me, and the sense of dread is so strong I try to get up again, but I just fall back down.

"Settle down, I said!"

"Where's Jimmy?"

"The guy they call Blood Bath?"

I nod. How does this guy know who Jimmy is? Does he know me, too?

"Is he all right?"

"He's fine. Or at least he should be. I left him in the parking lot, in the sun, so they couldn't get to him. And he was still alive. In fact, he was doing better than you, surprisingly."

I relax. If Jimmy's ok, then all I have to worry about is myself. And I can take care of myself. Then again, maybe I shouldn't take this guy's word for it. Who is he, and what does he want? Why aren't I dead?

"I should be dead."

He nods enthusiastically, like we were debating and I suddenly came over to his side.

"By all rights, definitely."

"So why am I not? Or am I dead? Am I gonna turn into a vampire now?"

I touch my neck, remembering how the vampire bit me. It's wrapped up in a thick bandage. I hadn't noticed that. He's chuckling.

"Nah, it takes more than that."

"Like what?"

"Well, there's a blood exchange thing, like, you need to drink their blood, and they have to drink a lot more of yours... it's all very sexy. In an exchange of bodily fluids way."

I make a face, and I don't even try to hide it. This guy is so many levels of gross.

"So, what, like, I have to agree?"

He shrugs.

"Depends. Not really. Let's just say you got lucky, this time."

"Did I?"

I was dead. There is no question about it. No kind of luck gets you out of a situation like that. I watch him as he grins at me. Is he trying to play me? His face is weird. I can't define his ethnicity. His skin is brown, but it's also very pale. His hair is a sort of dark, reddish chestnut, and almost curly, but not quite. He's pretty short, too, but stocky and muscular. He's got a stupid Emo haircut, but he's wearing jeans that look straight out of the grunge 1990s. His t-shirt has Big Bird printed on it, of all things, and his eyebrow is pierced. He says nothing for a long time, and shrugs.

"Ok, so maybe I helped you guys out a bit."

"You saying you killed those vampires? All by yourself?"

"Oh, no, they're still alive. Well, undead, anyway. I just wanted you out."

This guy's making less and less sense with every passing second. What could he want with me?

"Why?"

"Way to look a gift horse in the mouth, kid."

"I'm not a kid!"

He laughs. Is this guy out of his mind? I sit up straight. I don't care how much it hurts, or that I almost fall off the couch because of how dizzy it makes me; I just have to regain control of the conversation. He grins and shakes his head.

"Watch it. You're still pretty weak from the blood loss."

"I'm fine. Now tell me what I want to know."

I'm not fine, not really, but I need him to think I am. I drink my soda; the caffeine ought to keep me going. He shrugs dismissively.

"Suit yourself. What do you wanna know?"

I think about where to start again. How does he know about the vampires? How, and why did he get me out?

"Who are you?"

"I told you, you can call me Erik."

"That tells me your name, if that's even really it, but not who you are. Why did you help me? And how?"

He leans back comfortably on the couch, shrugging again, looking at the ceiling. It's old-fashioned, made entirely of wood.

"I have my reasons."

"Are you just going to taunt me by telling me to ask away, and then dodge my questions? Tell me what you know!"

He blinks, then squints at the ceiling, shrugging.

"I know a whole lot of things. For example, I know that if you cut worms in half, it doesn't really make two worms."

That's it. This guy's nuts. I'm getting out of here.

"Look, I don't know what kind of fucked up game you're playing with me here, but..."

I try to stand. Even supporting myself on the table, I don't make it more than a couple of inches off the couch before I crash over the table. The guy has the nerve to not only laugh, but to actually catch me before I hit the floor. He drops me back on the couch, like I weigh nothing. The pain makes me breathe hard, which is actually a vicious circle, because breathing hurts. I try to hit him, but he's already out of my reach. I concentrate on how much this jackass is pissing me off, and I manage to make a little flame in my hand, despite the weakness. He stops laughing, slowly.

"All right! All right! Calm down. I didn't mean to mess with you. You're just so easy to get a rise out of. I mean, you realize your questions are pretty vague, don't you?"

"Then start talking!"

He shakes his head.

"Look. Why don't I order some pizza? You must be hungry. Maybe the time it takes for it to come will be enough for you to cool down."

I can't take it anymore; I have to shout, no matter how much it hurts my ribs.

"I don't fucking want pizza! I want answers!"

"Then consider it a two for one special. Besides, you could see it this way: if you eat, you'll feel stronger, and then you can think straight enough to ask what you want."

I consider it. It seems like a sensible plan. I'm hungry as hell. I reach for the can of coke, but I spilt it when I fell on the table.

"Make it Chinese, and you've got a deal."

He grins, taking out a cell phone from his pocket.

"All right! Got a favorite place?"

I shrug.

"Any will do. But I like Fung Shing."

"What do you want?"

"Get me the BBQ pork."

He starts dialing on his cell phone. Instead of dialing with his thumb, he holds it in one hand and presses the buttons with the index of the other hand, and I can see he's dialing 411. He has a funny air of concentration as he asks for the number to Fung Shing, like he's afraid he's going to say the wrong thing. I think I must look a bit like that when I talk to Mister Lupino on the phone. When he's transferred to the restaurant, though, he seems perfectly relaxed and fluent when he makes his order in Mandarin, or Cantonese, or whatever kind of Chinese it is they speak over there.

I search my pockets. I still have my suit on, or what's left of it. It's mostly burnt off, now. Fortunately, my pack of cigarettes and phone are still in there, untouched. I light one, and check my phone. I have one missed call from Lupino, three from Jimmy; I guess he must really be all right. I check my messages anyway just to make sure, and hang up once I hear his voice screaming curses at my voicemail. I think about returning Lupino's call, but I see it's almost midnight, and he's probably been in bed for a long time already.

He's done his conversation then, and he actually has to look for the red button to hang up.

"All right, food's on the way."

"So now you'll answer my questions?"

He laughs again.

"You gotta learn how to relax. You're way too stressed for someone your age."

Here he goes again, bringing my age into it.

"You said you would answer."

"I said you could ask."

I glare at him, and I'm about to tell him what I think of his little word games when he raises his hands disarmingly.

"All right, all right, I'll do my best. But you could be a little more trusting of people, I mean, I did bring you into my home, you know. I could have left you there to die."

"There's a place to start. Why didn't you?"

"Well, you're a special guy, Alex Winters."

It doesn't come as a surprise that he knows who I am. After all, he knew who Jimmy was. But I don't know how much he knows, so I try not to give anything away.

"Why do you say that?"

He grins at me again, leaning back comfortably. He's facing me, but there's a weird, sideways quality to his expression.

"Come on. Everyone who's anyone in this town knows about what you can do."

I think about it. I have kind of been flaunting my power, but it's the only real way I have to assert my authority.

"All right, fair enough. So, what, you saved me 'cause you need me to do you a favor or something?"

"Not exactly."

"Then what do you want from me?"

"Nothing. Well, that's not true. I want you to stay away from the vampires."

"What? Why?"

"Because you're a big advantage to have. And I can't let them have you."

I stare at him. It sounds almost reasonable. And I can't say the idea of fighting vampires is the most appealing one I've ever had, but he doesn't understand my predicament. Also, it raises a lot more questions.

There's a knock on the door, and he gets up to go answer. There's talking, and he comes back with a brown paper bag. He puts it down on the table as he sits, and pushes it over to my side. I open it, grab the plastic fork inside, and tear the Styrofoam container open. There's another can of coke in there too. I've shoveled half the contents in my mouth by the time I realize he's not eating.

"Where's your food?"

"I ate already."

"So are you gonna tell me who you are, or are you just gonna keep saying creepy things that just barely hint at how much you're leaving out?"

He chuckles again, like I said something cute.

"I am called Erik. My hobbies include watching Spanish soap operas and listening to Wagner."

I roll my eyes, but I'm used to it by now. He probably thinks he's clever. I reach for the new can of coke, pop it open and drink before I answer, to give him a chance to say something a little more helpful. He doesn't.

"Stop fucking with me. You know what I want to know."

"Well, I'm also not a mind-reader, which you're obviously assuming."

"What's your interest in all this?"

He leans forward, putting his elbows on his knees and shrugging a little bit.

"Call me a concerned citizen."

"A citizen who can just waltz into a vampire den and rescue a guy with super powers?"

He has a smile that seems mischievous. He's fucking with me again, and he's having too much fun doing it.

"A concerned citizen."

"Right."

I shake my head. I put down the empty Styrofoam container and pick up the coke again, trying to make a mental list of what I've managed to gather so far. He knows who I am. He knows who Jimmy is. He knows what I can do, and he wants me on his side, or at least, he doesn't want me on the vampires' side. Either way, he's got a side, which means he's involved on some level. He's also capable, or else I would certainly be dead, and possibly so would he.

That's a pretty short list, and one that raises more questions than it answers, really. But it's obvious he's not willing to tell me anything useful.

"Is there anything you will tell me?"

He nods again, enthusiastically.

"Yes. Stay away from them. They're more dangerous than you think, even now. It's really not like a monster movie. There's no climactic moment in which you realize their weaknesses and kill them all. They're strong, and they're vicious, and you're nothing but food for them. And if you even think about fighting them again, call me. Have you lost my card?"

I check in the cigarette case.

"No, I still got it."

"Good. It's my cell phone, so you can reach me on it pretty much all the time. And I sleep at odd hours, so don't be afraid to call, anytime. Just don't leave me voice mail. I never take my messages."

"So, you're asking me to stay away from them, but you're not expecting me to?"

He shrugs with a derisive little smirk.

"I'm just a realist. It's important not to delude oneself."

"Sure."

He gets up off the couch.

"All right. I suppose I should get you a pillow and blanket, and something else to wear. You should get some actual sleep."

I sigh. I don't know if I'm going to be able to get any sleep in this place. It's unfamiliar, and I have too many things to worry about. There is one thing that would help, though.

"Hey, where's your TV?"

He scratches his head.

"Hmm... I got one upstairs... I don't have cable, though."

"Doesn't matter."

"All right, let's go."

He comes next to me and all but lifts me by putting an arm under my good shoulder, and takes me up the stairs. I try to stand to show him I don't need him, but as soon as I've taken two steps I get dizzy and start to fall, so I let him help me walk. There's wallpaper everywhere, and the one in the hall is yellow and gold, with hints of brown. It has flowers on it, as well.

"Man, your place is ugly."

"What are you talking about? It's the height of fashion!"

"Yeah, maybe forty years ago."

He looks offended, but doesn't answer. He takes me to a bedroom where the queen-sized bed is unmade. There are clothes on the floor, but nothing dramatic, one pair of pants and two or three t-shirts. He helps me settle down on the left side of the bed. It's a little more comfortable than the couch, and the food has given me enough strength to arrange my own pillows.

There's a small, old-fashioned TV with knobs instead of buttons next to the door, in front of the bed. It's hooked up to a couple of video game consoles, at least all the ones that Luke bought for the kids, and then some. Some of them look pretty old, all boxy and square and gray. He turns on the TV, and fiddles with the antennas. There's a blurry, snowy picture of an old movie I don't know. He turns up the volume.

"Don't. Can you mute that TV?"

"Mute?"

"Yeah."

"Sure, I guess."

He looks at me for a few moments more to see if I'm going to explain myself, but I'm certainly not going to give him the satisfaction. He finally shrugs, and turns the volume knob down to the minimum.

"All right, I'll let you get some sleep. I'll be downstairs if you need me."

AUGUST 30TH, 8:51 AM

    The TV is still on and I'm alone in bed when I wake up. I still feel a little dizzy, and nauseous, but I'm definitely a lot stronger than I was when I went to sleep. The room is dark, and I can't see any light through the curtains. I try to sit up, and when that works, I try to stand up. That works too, except for a mild tingling in my legs like they've been asleep too long. I walk to the window, and pull the curtains open. At first I'm not sure what I'm looking at, and then I realize the windows have been painted black on the inside. Sunlight is showing through the places where the paint is thinnest.

    That's just weird. What's wrong with this guy? Could he be one of them? Wouldn't he hurt me, if he was? It's not like he's lacked the opportunity.

    I grab my cell phone, and call Jimmy. I'm expecting to have to leave a message on his voice mail, but to my surprise, he actually answers.

    "Boss? That you?"

    "It's me. You all right?"

    "I'm fine! What about you? That thing started eating you and then some guy threw me out a window and I passed out! I thought for sure you'd be dead!"

He sounds relieved, and I can't help but smile. Of all the guys who work for me, Jimmy might be the only one who truly doesn't want me dead in some part of his being.

"I'm all right. Some guy helped me. I think it was the same guy who threw you out the window. Can you come pick me up?"

"Sure, where are you?"

I open my mouth to say, and I suddenly realize I have no clue where I am.

"Uh, actually, I'll call you right back. In the meantime, can you swing by the house and pick me up a suit again? The one I have is all burnt."

I hang up, and walk out of the room slowly. My legs still feel wobbly, so I have to lean heavily on the railing when I go down the stairs so I don't fall. I'm stronger, but I'm definitely weak enough to be scared a couple times.

He's in the living room when I get downstairs, sitting on the couch reading a book that looks really old. He looks up when I come in, even though I'm real quiet, and closes his book, leaving a finger between the pages to mark his spot.

"Feeling better, I see."

"Yeah. Much. Ready to go home. Thanks."

He nods.

"Good."

"So... what's your address? I'd have my ride pick me up here."

He smirks at me, and puts down the open book on the table.

"337 Walker."

I search my brain. Walker. Where did I hear that?

"In Old Town?"

"That's right."

He's three blocks away from the magic shop. Jimmy ought to know where it is. I pick up my phone and dial while Erik stands and vanishes in the direction of the kitchen. I glance down at what he's reading, but it's in a weird language I can't understand, on top of being hand written. Who the hell buys hand written books, anyways? If it's some kind of journal, it certainly ain't his; the writing is faded, and obviously ancient.

Jimmy doesn't pick up, so I figure he must be driving or in the house, and I leave a message with the address. He might take it or call me back, either way, it works. I hang up and look around.

There's lots of bookcases here. I hadn't noticed them last night, busy as I was trying to find out what was happening to me. All the books on the shelves look really old. I recognize some Latin and Chinese, but most are in languages I've never seen before. He's still not back, so I try to follow him where he went. I walk through a dining room that could have been pulled straight out of a Jane Austen movie adaptation, with high back chairs, a large dark wooden table and decorative moldings on the walls and ceiling, and into a kitchen that looks like it was decorated in the fifties. The few appliances are oddly round, and yellow, and they look vintage, no imitations. There is an island counter in the middle, and all around it are round, red leatherette stools. He's leaning against it, pushing down the filter of a small French press coffee maker, concentration painted all over his face. He looks up at me when he's done, grinning.

"Made you some coffee. You do like coffee, don't you?"

He looks uncertain, suddenly. I think it's a little funny.

"Yeah, coffee's fine."

I sit down, and he frowns at his fridge, then looks back at me.

"I don't have any milk. I'm pretty sure I have sugar somewhere, though."

"It's all right. I like it black."

He nods and takes out a cup, pouring come coffee into it, then slides it over to me. He doesn't pour one for himself. I pick it up, and look at it before drinking. It has a faded picture of Homer Simpson eating a donut on it. The coffee's very strong, and I feel the caffeine jolting me awake on the first sip.

"You're not having any?"

"Not a big coffee fan."

"Fair enough. So, what's with the blacked out windows?"

He shrugs dismissively.

"Like I said, I sleep at odd hours."

I watch him for a bit, and then I decide to be direct about it. After all, he's the one who said my questions were vague.

"So, are you a vampire?"

He blinks at me stupidly for a few seconds, then bursts out laughing.

"You know, you should be careful what you ask."

"Hey. You're the one that told me to be direct."

I drink some more coffee, looking at him over the cup. He chuckles again, and shakes his head.

"I like you, kid. Sorry. I mean Alex. You've got guts."

"Well, yeah."

If he knows anything about me, he should know at least that. You don't get to be where I am at my age without stepping on some massively dangerous toes. He goes to open a cupboard next to the fridge.

"You hungry? I got Twinkies."

"Got anything else?"

The cupboard seems pretty empty. He stands on tiptoes to see the higher shelves; he is a pretty short guy. He reaches in and retrieves a small can from the top shelf, squinting at it suspiciously.

"I got canned tuna. Why do I have canned tuna? Oh, never mind. That's been expired a while."

He puts the can back in the cupboard, and my phone rings; it's Jimmy.

"Yeah?"

"Boss? I'm parked outside."

"I'm on my way."

I hang up, and look up at my strange host.

"My ride's here."

"Good. Well. Have a nice trip home. And don't forget to call."

"I don't suppose you'll walk me out into the sunlit front yard?"

He just smiles, and picks up the mug I left on the counter.

"I'm sure you'll find the exit by yourself."

I do. The house is in a nice part of Old Town, small and surrounded by tall trees. Like most of the buildings in that part of the city, it's at least one or two hundred years old. From the outside, I see that all the windows of the house, at least all the ones I can see, have been blacked out.

Jimmy is parked in the driveway. He examines the house as I get in on the passenger side. He looks sleepy. His hair is ruffled and messed up, and his clothes look slept in.

"So what is this place, man? What happened to you?"

"It's kind of complicated. Come on, let's get going, I'll explain on the way."

AUGUST 30TH, 1:17 PM

Jimmy slows down in front of the house where the kids live, and pulls in the driveway. He turns off the motor, and then looks at me. He took me to his place so I could shower and change before coming back here, and he's been moody ever since our conversation about the weird vampire dude. He's said nothing since we left his place, which isn't necessarily unusual in and of itself, except for the scowl.

"You really gonna listen to this guy? Do as he told you?"

I stare at him. So that's why he's mad. He's got it all wrong.

"Don't be an idiot. Have I ever done anything I'm told?"

"I dunno, man. When Lupino says jump..."

"Don't bring Lupino into this."

"Well, whatever you say."

"Look. If this guy wants me to stay out of it, then he's obviously involved, isn't he? And if he doesn't want these guys to have me, he's not on their side, and if he can just waltz in and get the both of us out of a situation like yesterday morning's fight, then maybe he'll take care of it for us."

"Yeah, and reap the benefits."

"I don't think he's interested in that so much."

Jimmy looks at me for a long time, like he's making up his mind, and then he just sighs and shakes his head.

"I don't know about this, Alex. I don't think you should trust this guy."

"I don't trust him. But I think I know where he's headed, and I think it's in our best interest to let it play out. For now."

"All right. Well, I guess I better let you get some rest."

"Go see the clubs that haven't been affected, and put protection on them. Actual protection."

"Already done."

I nod.

"It's good I got you, Jimmy."

"It's good we got each other. Well. You know. Not in a gay way."

I hit him on the shoulder as I laugh and step out of the car.

"Yeah, yeah. Don't worry. Call me if you got anything new."

I walk to the house, and he drives away as I open the front door. It's pretty empty inside. There's no one either in the game room or the living room, and I can't see the inside of the kitchen from here but it's quiet. I start making my way up the stairs, and I hear steps running from the kitchen towards me. I almost stop, thinking it must be Luke, but then I hear Lori's voice.

"Alex! Stop!"

I walk faster, but she catches up to me, appearing at the bottom of the stairs. When she sees that I saw her, she plants her fists on her hips and glares at me.

"You owe me a talk."

"I don't owe you anything."

I reach the first floor landing, and I go on to the second. She can't see me anymore, so she runs up the stairs after me. I go even faster, but I start feeling dizzy, and I have to stop. She catches up to me, a little out of breath, and I hate her at that moment, for making me run away from a girl who's smaller than me and just wants to talk. I have to lean against the wall so I don't fall down the stairs, and when she gets a closer look at me, she slows down, frowning. She reaches to touch me, like she's going to help, and I stand again, no matter how much the room is spinning.

"What happened to you? Alex!"

"Nothing. I'm fine. Go away."

With a firm grip on the railing, I finally reach the third floor, though by now I'm breathing pretty hard, and I'm painfully reminded of the pain in my ribs; I really must have broken a couple of them. I have to lean on the wall with my good arm to make it to my room, and once I'm there, I don't have any strength to struggle with the door and Lori, so I just go sit on my bed. She closes the door behind her and comes closer. I think she's going to sit on the bed next to me, so I lie down and make sure I'm taking up too much room for that to happen. She stops, and grabs the chair to pull it closer and sit on it.

"Go away, Lori."

"No way. Like I said, you owe me a talk."

"I owe you nothing."

I try to turn to show her my back, but that forces me to roll on my bad shoulder, and it hurts too much, so I just don't look at her instead.

"You said we could talk when I was sober. Well, I am."

"Yeah, well that changed when I found out you roofied me."

She has the decency to look ashamed and shut up, even if her silence doesn't last too long.

"Well, it's not like you passed out and I did things to you. I just gave you a little, to loosen you up, and that's all it did!"

I feel myself snarling at her, and I can't help it.

"You had no right!"

"Luke already gave me the speech. You're fine, and all that happened is we had a lot of fun."

I don't really know what to say to that, so I keep giving her my best pissed off look and say nothing.

"Come on, Alex! You have to admit it was fun!"

"How could I? I don't even remember!"

She frowns at me, and looks down.

"Look, Alex, I'm sorry. I didn't know what else to do. You never want to talk to me. You're so distant! Every time something meaningful happens, you just retreat into yourself and don't talk to anyone about it. I wanted to have a real conversation with you. That's all."

"I remember you talking with your mouth."

I frown as I say it. What else would she talk with?

"Well. You know. Not with words."

She shrugs, and looks at me with a shy smile, but a real smile, not the sly look she has when she's trying to be sexy. It forces her whole mouth to move up on her face, pressing dimples above the corners of her lips, making her cheeks rounder and her eyes squint up happily. I look away quickly; it makes it hard to hold on to my anger.

"Some things can only really be said without words."

She reaches to take my hand, and I think about flinching away, but it's more an afterthought than an urge. I don't want to look at her, though. Not while I'm trying to stay mad at her. Her hand is a bit cold, but it feels kind of good anyway to be holding it.

She doesn't say any more, and I don't know what to say, either. I never know what to say to girls. I'm not even really sure what I want or don't want with her anymore. I know I want something, but I know I don't want to have to talk about it.

I look back at her, because I don't know what else to do, and there's a look in her face, like she wants the same thing I want, and I can't help but panic a little. She leans down, bringing her face closer to mine, and mercifully, my phone rings. I scramble away from her and reach into my pocket to grab my cell so fast that it slips out of my hands and falls to the floor. I get up quickly, and my shoulder and ribs hurt like hell, slowing my movements. By the time I pick it up again, I've missed the call, and it's from Lupino, too. She's staring at me, but her eyes are laughing. I get up on the other side of the bed, and start dialing. I stop before I make the call, though, 'cause I'm not sure what to say, and I call my voicemail instead.

There's the messages that Jimmy left me yesterday, asking me where I am and if I'm alive, and there are two messages from Mister Lupino. The first one just asks me to call him back. The second one, though, sounds a bit more serious.

"Alex, this is Domenic Lupino. I did not hear back from you yesterday. I hope everything is all right. I am expecting to hear from you today."

I erase the message and hang up the phone. Lori's still sitting on the chair, smiling at me, but I'm standing on the other side of the bed, and things seem clearer from this distance.

"Um, Lori, I gotta return this call. It's important."

She pouts, sighs, and gets up.

"Fine. But I'm not giving up, Alex. I'll be back."

She walks out of the room, and I try to ignore what she said as I call Mister Lupino. It only takes him two rings to pick up.

"Yes, hello?"

"Mister Lupino? It's..."

"Alex! Good to finally hear from you. Is everything all right?"

"It's fine. Just a little bit of trouble."

It's good that I can't really say anything involved over the phone, since I'm calling his land line. He has a burner cell like I do, but he doesn't use it unless he has to, because he says it'll give him cancer.

"Hmm. Nothing too serious, I trust?"

"Not really."

"When will I see you?"

I try to think. I've sent Jimmy off with some work to do, and there's no way he'll be back early enough to give me a ride. I have to learn how to drive.

"Uh, tomorrow morning?"

"Good! For breakfast?"

I remember he eats pretty early. Jimmy's just going to have to be up at this time. Maybe it'll be a good occasion to ask him to teach me how to drive.

"I'll be there."

"Good. I will see you then."

I hang up, and look at the door to my room. It's open, and there doesn't seem to be anyone just beyond it. I go lock it anyway, just to make sure I'm not disturbed anymore.

AUGUST 30TH, 10:16 PM

I'm starving when I wake up. I look at the time and see it's pretty late, and thankfully, just past curfew. I check Luke's office before I head down the stairs. He's not there, but there is light, so I know he's around somewhere.

I'm real quiet as I pass the first floor, and nobody seems to have heard me. I light a cigarette when I'm downstairs, with a lighter, 'cause I'm too weak and too hungry to make the fire myself. The light in the kitchen is on, so I approach with caution, but it's only Luke, cooking something in a pan over the stove. He looks up at me when I'm almost through the door.

"Hey, Alex. I was wondering when you were finally going to come out of your room."

"Fell asleep. What're you cooking?"

"Grilled cheese. Want one?"

"Sure."

I sit at the counter, 'cause the big cafeteria table we have for meals has been folded and put away next to the wall. Luke gets a couple of plates. He puts the grilled cheese sandwich he had been cooking in one, and hands it to me before turning to the fridge and retrieving the white bread and radioactive orange processed cheese in individually wrapped slices.

The sandwich is greasy and piping hot, just the way I like it. It's probably what my mom made us the most often at home. That, and macaroni and cheese. I don't eat them often, because I had way too much of it when I was a kid, but once in a while, I get a mean craving for them.

"Thanks, man. It's real good."

He nods, putting his assembled sandwich on the pan.

"I had dinner with the kids, but I'm working late and I skipped lunch, so I got hungry..."

"Yeah. I kinda skipped eating, today."

He looks sideways at me, and makes a face before looking back down at the pan.

"I wasn't gonna say anything... but you look like death. Are you ok?"

"I'm fine. I just... lost some blood."

"Again? You should be careful. And you shouldn't be skipping meals. Here. Eat that one too. I'll order you some real food."

He dumps the second sandwich in my plate, and goes to a cupboard over the fridge to retrieve the menus we accumulate there. He starts leafing through them without asking me what I want to eat. I'm used to it by now, though. I know if he's deciding for me, it's because he thinks I need something specific and he just wants to make sure I get it. I eat the second sandwich while he picks up the wireless phone and orders us an obscene amount of hamburgers, no fries. I'm through eating by the time he's done ordering, and I still feel so hungry I have to fight the urge to pick up the plate and lick it.

"Should be here in half an hour."

"Burgers?"

"You like those, don't you? Red meat is just the thing for you right now."

I nod, and he finally makes himself a grilled cheese sandwich. I watch him, wanting to ask for more, but I control myself, because I have food on the way.

I hear the front door open, and jerk my head towards it even though I can't see it from where I'm sitting. I look at Luke, but he's craning his neck to see the door too, so I get up, ready to defend my territory. I hear Lori's voice then, and I almost stop. I don't know who she's talking to, but she knows them, and I'd rather not have her notice that I'm around. Then, another voice answers her, and an alarm bell rings in my mind. It's Mark. I can see Luke getting ready to scold, and I step in front of him, motioning for him to stay back.

"Come on! Aren't we friends?"

"You know it's nothing to do with friendship, Lori. It's the business. I can't talk to you about it."

"You can trust me!"

I lean against the wall on the side of the kitchen door, peeking in carefully. She's in the entrance, talking to Mark through the door. He looks the same, but there's something about his attitude that betrays the change in him. Also, he's standing outside. Why isn't he coming in? He's not alone; there's a couple guys with him that I don't recognize. They're all standing outside, like they're being polite.

"Well, can we come in, then?"

The next few seconds feel kind of like they happen in slow motion, and I can see everything that's happening, but I'm going as slow as they are. I see Lori open her mouth to answer, and I shout to stop her. But the yes escapes her lips at the same time as I shout my warning, and by the time she's registered I'm speaking to her, Mark is stepping through the threshold, and I just know that I'm right, that something is wrong with him. I rush over to the entrance as he comes in, followed by the guys with him. I'm almost there when he grabs Lori by the back of the neck and yanks her toward him, his face changing. The teeth don't grow, exactly; it's more like everything that makes his face monstrous just comes into focus. Lori screams when she sees it, and he bites her.

One of the guys makes it past Lori and Mark, lunging at me. But Lori's in danger, and, strangely enough, it brings the anger to my mind instantaneously, making me feel nearly invincible. The fire roars out of my hands at the vampire, engulfing him completely. I hold it there until he bursts into ashes, and I see the other three hesitate. I take advantage of their pause to rush to the vampire biting Lori. I grab her arm with my left hand, and push the vampire that used to be Mark away with my injured right arm, pushing flames at him in a way that I hope won't hurt her. He screams and recoils, and I catch her. I hold her awkwardly in my left arm, and I use the right to make a wall of fire between them and me. I feel someone trying to take Lori, and I nearly attack, but I think to look and see it's only Luke.

"Is she ok?"

He looks her over quickly and nods.

"She's alive. She'll be fine."

"All right."

I try to think of what to do. I can't keep up the wall of fire forever. For one, the walls are starting to get burned, and the wood that supports their structure will start catching fire soon. I can't fight them all at once, either, and I'm the only one here that can stand up to them. And if I let a single one get past me, then some of the kids upstairs are going to die. There are service stairs at the back of the house, though, that used to serve to vanish a politician or two in the days of the brothel.

"Luke, get all the kids out through the back stairs. If you see anyone else outside, wait for me inside at the back door, ok?"

He nods, and runs up the stairs, leaving Lori there. She doesn't look conscious, so I'm sure she'd have slowed him down. I keep watching the vampires, concentrating on my firewall. They're grinning at me with their too-sharp teeth, trying to find a way through my fire. I don't like their confidence. I don't have enough strength to keep it up anymore, but I know Luke hasn't had enough time yet, so I keep pushing, and pushing, with all I've got. The flames get too thin, eventually, and one of them is able to leap over the wall to tackle me. I dodge him, but I have to drop the flames, and as soon as he sees the other vampires moving, he heads for Lori. I'm closer to her than he is, though, so I put myself on his path, and reach for what I have left of rage and hatred to hurl all the fire I can summon up at him. It barely breaks his stride, but once he's grabbed me, he can't hold on for more than a second or so, he never gets a chance to get close enough for me to see if his fucked up teeth are sharp enough to tear through the tape and gauze my neck is still wrapped in, before he explodes, sending ash and embers in my face.

I spit out vampire ash and have a fleeting thought of how disgusting that is before I get back up on my feet. They're inches away from me, stopped by the flames, but not for long. I cover myself in fire, making sure my clothes are well caught, and barrel through them to get to Lori. I have to protect her; she's my responsibility. I quench the flames all around me so as to not burn her when we touch, and I throw myself over her, covering her. It's not hard, really. She's much smaller than I am. As soon as I'm on top of her, I start the fire on my back, and build it up in a roaring explosion that fills the whole room, keeping it up for as long as I can, covering her face and hair with my arms to make sure she doesn't get burned.

When the anger and the fire drain from me completely, I'm panting, and I can barely lift myself up. My clothes, or what's left of them, are still on fire, but I feel calm enough to extinguish it. Mercifully, Lori is starting to come around. She blinks up at me, then looks at something beyond me that seems to terrify her, and she has a little strangled gasp like she's not quite able to shout. I turn around instantly, adrenaline rushing to my heart, expecting to see more vampires, but I can't see anyone moving anywhere, and the floor is covered with a thin dusting of ash. It's only then that I notice what scared her: the walls have finally really caught, and the house is burning. It's only fire, though; that, I can deal with. I struggle to my feet, the relief washing away the adrenaline I need to keep going. I have to lean on a wall to get my balance, and it collapses beneath my weight. Lori catches me before I fall, and I lean on her as she helps me towards the back door, through the kitchen.

I try to extinguish the fire, but there's too much, and I'm too weak. I just hope there aren't any vampires waiting for us in the back yard. When we get there, though, I see Luke getting the kids in the mini-bus I got them last year. They're all in their pajamas, still, scared and cold, staring at me and Lori as Luke tries to get them to climb on the bus. The youngest are already sitting inside, their faces pressed against the glass, gawking, and I realize that most of my clothes have burned off, and I'm nearly naked. I don't have my cell anymore, either. I hope Luke had the presence of mind to grab the emergency bag from the safe.

I let go of Lori and get myself in the bus, leaning heavily on the metal railing and the front bench to pull myself up on the first available seat. As Lori gets in after I do, I notice that Kim is standing next to me, offering me a pink blanket with Hello Kitty printed all over it. She's one of the youngest ones, only about nine or ten or so, but the look she gives me is serious, haunted, even. I don't want to put soot and blood on her blanket, but I have nothing else to cover myself with, so I take it and try to be careful. She goes away without a word, and Lori takes a seat next to me. Luke finally climbs in too. He takes a moment to stare at the house. It's obviously burning now, the inside glowing faintly red and yellow under the black smoke. He tosses something at me and I catch it before realizing that it's the emergency bag I put in the safe after the first attempt on my life. He gets behind the wheel as I open it, and looks at me over his shoulder as he turns the key in the ignition.

"Where do we go?"

I look up from the bag to stare at him stupidly. I have no idea where I should take them. We have about twelve kids here, of whom we're obviously not the parents. We might be able to pass them off as some kind of sports team, but not when all of them are wearing their pajamas and have no luggage. It's the middle of the night, too, so there's nowhere I can buy them clothes. If I show up with this lot at a hotel, they'll call the cops for sure, and then I'm looking at a world of complications.

"Uh... just drive, for now. Give me a few minutes."

He nods and puts the bus in first gear, pulling out of the parking lot. I pick up the burner phone in the bag, and use it to dial 911 so the fire department can salvage what there is to be saved from the house. I don't linger on the phone with them, just make sure they're on their way, and then I move on to slightly less urgent problems.

I start to dial Jimmy's phone number, and don't send the call. What would Jimmy do? Even if he did accept to have others in his home, which he barely tolerates me seeing, he's got a tiny-ass one bedroom apartment. And he wouldn't know what to do; he's barely able to keep taking care of himself. There's Lupino. But it's late, and he'll probably be sleeping. Besides, what would he do? He'd have nowhere to put us but his own home, and there's no way I'd impose on him like that. Where else is there?

I stare at my phone and think furiously. Luke is driving slowly, and he keeps shooting me little looks to see if I've made up my mind about what to do yet. Where else is there? Who can give us a roof for the night, at least until I get them clothes so we don't look so damn suspicious?

Lori hands me the silver cigarette case. I stare at it, dumbfounded. I have no idea how, when and where she got it. I certainly didn't think of it, but I'm so happy to see it now that I would hug her, if it wasn't way too awkward. I open it to grab a smoke from it, and notice the weird, wrinkled business card stuck under my three remaining cigarettes. That guy had a house. It was pretty big. So, he's probably a vampire, but he didn't seem that bad, and if I'm there, and Luke is there, we can keep an eye on him, and be out of there as soon as we got stuff for the kids to wear. I dial the number. The phone rings once, twice, three times, and then I hear a lot of confused, muffled sounds for at least ten seconds before his voice.

"Hello?"

"Hi. It's Alex Winters."

"Ah. So you decided not to heed my warning, then?"

"Not exactly by my choice. Your friends attacked my house. Now I need a place to stay for the night."

There's silence at the other end. I let him take in my meaning. It takes him at least twenty seconds to answer, so I know he's aware of what I want and he's just playing dumb.

"...so?"

"So, I need to borrow your house for the night."

He sighs.

"This isn't exactly the kind of help I had in mind. My house isn't a hotel."

"Well, we're coming anyway."

"We? There's more than you?"

"Yeah. And we need a place to stay. It's just for the night, we'll be gone in the morning, and you don't have to feed us or anything. But you are going to do this for me, because you're involved in this shit, and I'm holding you responsible."

I hear him hesitate, then click his tongue and sigh again.

"Aren't you a mobster? Don't you have lots of money to go to a hotel?"

"It's not a question of money. I can give you money. We need a place that's question-free. Now."

"...fine. One night. And you're out in the morning."

"We'll be there in fifteen minutes."

I hang up before he has a chance to change his mind, and look up at Luke.

"We're headed to Old Town. 337 Walker."

He nods, turns the bus right on the next street so we're headed in the right direction, and I can finally light my cigarette and relax.

AUGUST 31ST, 12:03 AM

The look on Erik's face is absolutely priceless when the bus pulls into his driveway. He's standing outside, on his lawn, his mouth hanging open when he sees me come down the steps. I can walk by myself again, and I'm holding the Hello Kitty blanket wrapped around my waist. He looks me up and down, looks at the kids on the bus, and shakes his head.

"All right. Just get inside and try not to attract attention."

He goes back in his house, leaving the door open behind him. I turn to Luke.

"Make sure they all get in, and lock the door behind you."

I get inside the house. It badly needs to be repainted on the outside; the original color of the wood is showing almost everywhere. I can't see him anywhere. This isn't starting well; I'd decided I wasn't going to let him out of my sight for a second, and here I am for three minutes and I've already lost him. I don't have to search too long, though. After I've looked through the living room and kitchen, and some of the kids have started to come in, I hear him coming down the stairs. He's carrying a pile of folded blankets made of gray and red felted wool. He puts them down on one of the leather couches, and I notice there's some clothes folded on top. He hands them to me. It's a faded black t-shirt of some band I never heard of, called Nirvana, and a pair of jeans that are too wide and too short, but they're clothes, and they'll do until the morning, anyway. I put them on then and there.

When I'm done, I notice he's watching the kids come in one after the other. The young ones are all sleepy, and already looking for a place to lie down.

"There's a guest room upstairs with a double bed. I also have a king-sized bed in my room. I'm sure there's enough room for all of them to lie down."

I'm not sure I want any of them in his room, but they look so exhausted, I can't say no. Luke is coming in, and he locks the door behind him like I asked.

"Luke, can you take some of them upstairs to go to sleep? There's a couple rooms with beds in them."

He nods, and starts rounding up the youngest ones, leaving with about half of them. The rest find places on the couches or on the floors, and Lori starts distributing blankets, and the brown and orange pillows from the couch. I notice the ugly, mangled wound on her neck. It seems to not be bleeding anymore but still had time to stain the front and side of her white, fur collar coat, and the sight of it gives me a sudden, sickening, sinking feeling that brings the taste of bile to my lips and turns my knees into water, forcing me to sit down on the narrow table in the hallway. I let her get hurt. Worse than that, they were only there because of me. They could have killed all of them.

"You all right?"

Erik is making a weird face at me, frowning and squinting at the same time. I want to look up at him and tell him I'm fine, but I can't. I need a few more moments to gather myself.

"Can you make me some coffee?"

"You sure that's all you need?"

"Got any food?"

"Same as last time."

"All right, just the coffee."

He disappears into the kitchen. I find myself watching Lori. I'm incapable of taking my eyes off her. She sees me watching, and misunderstands the reason, smiling coyly at me before continuing to hand out the blankets. I find the strength in my legs to get up, and join Erik in the kitchen. He's brewing coffee as requested, and I just go sit at his counter. He watches me while his hands are busy pouring the hot water in the French press, but once he's still, his eyes fall on the infusing coffee.

"So, all these kids..."

I look at him warily. I can find reserves of strength in me to fight if need be. But the way he looks at me, he doesn't seem to be about to start something.

"...they're yours?"

What does he mean?

"They're their own people."

"I mean... you take care of them."

I shrug. He pushes the press down slowly, trapping the grains of coffee at the bottom.

"I guess."

He reaches into his cupboard and pulls out an old faded mug with a weird eighties-looking logo on it that says Doctor Who, filling it with black coffee. He looks me in the eye when he passes it over, though, not to say something, but like he's looking for something in me.

"Any particular reason?"

"Well... they're my responsibility."

"I think some of them are older than you are."

"Luke looks after them. He doesn't count. And Lori... What's your point, anyway?"

"My point is... Ok, I don't know what my point is. But do you think you're doing good by staying involved?"

Who the hell does that guy think he is?

"What fucking business is it of yours, anyway?"

"What, you mean apart from my house suddenly being turned into a home for wayward youths?"

"It's just for the night. And they're not... wayward, whatever that means. Besides, we were attacked!"

"Oh? So the vampires were after them, too?"

He's saying this is my fault. Like I don't know. I get up from my seat and grab him by the collar, slamming him against the counter.

"What the fuck do you know?!?"

He doesn't do anything to counter attack, only stares at me for a while and then looks over my shoulder. I turn around and notice Lori's standing there, looking at me with an expression I haven't seen on her face since the time I freed her from the brothel. I forgot how young she still is, how vulnerable and frail she can look.

"Alex? You're scaring the kids."

I'm scaring her, too. I let go of Erik, glaring at him meaningfully. It makes him smile, of all things, and I try to contain my rage when I turn to Lori. I'm not that good at doing that, though.

"It's fine. Go back to the living room."

She looks between me and Erik hesitantly, and I notice the wound on her neck again. My anger vanishes.

"Hey, Erik, have you got a first aid kit?"

"Somewhere, I guess."

"Go get it."

I don't look at him, but I hear him walk out of the kitchen. I grab a towel that's hanging on the oven door handle, and go to Lori. I lead her to a seat around the island counter, and I give her the towel to press against her neck. She doesn't look at me. She's pale; I hope it's more from the fear than the blood loss. I pick up the burner phone again to 411 a deli that delivers pastrami and order ridiculous quantities of it. When I hang up, I notice that the back of my hand has blood on it. Her blood.

She looks up over my head and I notice that Erik is there with his first aid kit. He puts it down on the counter and starts digging through it.

"I have some disinfectant here, and some gauze."

He pulls out a couple of glass bottles, and some yellowed bandages. They look old; so does the bag, for that matter.

"Uh... you sure these things are still good?"

He looks at me like I'm stupid for a second, then frowns at the bottles.

"What, these things expire?"

"Well, yeah, I guess, everything expires. Go find my friend Luke. He'll sort this out. He's the one with the glasses."

I watch him leave, and I have a thought about Luke's safety. I'm pretty sure this guy's a vampire. Even if he is, though, I feel sure I'm not in much danger. I can't exactly explain it, but as long as I stay awake to keep an eye over things I'm sure nothing will go wrong, even after everything else that's happened.

Lori's looking at me with her vulnerable face again, and I can't stand it. I don't know why I sent Erik and didn't go myself. What possessed me to let myself be trapped alone with her? She doesn't say anything, thankfully. I go to open the fridge to see if there's anything to drink in there. There's nothing, though, not even shelves. There's a white, unidentified cooler there, and under it, a 24-pack of bottled beer. I'm about to reach in and check what's inside the cooler when I hear steps. I close the door and look up to see Luke and Erik coming into the kitchen. Luke goes to look at Lori's neck right away, gently taking the towel from her hands. It's bloody, but not too bad. I can't tell by the amount of blood on the towel, but Luke will tell me if the bleeding is under control.

Luke looks at the bag on the table, and the bottles and gauze, and makes a face like he just noticed the bread he was eating was green.

"Is that seriously your first aid kit?"

"What's wrong with it?"

Luke goes to look at the contents of the bag. Erik watches him. Is he pouting?

"What's wrong with it! Did you steal it from a war museum, or did it come with the house? It looks at least fifty years old!"

"Well...! I... I guess I don't use it much."

Erik looks halfway between offended and ashamed. Luke sighs, and looks at me.

"Go get the kit that's in the bus. Make it quick."

I start to raise my eyebrows and plant my feet; no one tells me what to do, not even Luke. But I understand the urgency of the situation, and I say nothing. I walk out to the bus, still parked crookedly across the driveway. Luke left the door open, so I climb in. The bag from the safe is still on the front seat, slightly open. There's five thousand bucks cash in there, along with a gun and burner phone, for emergencies like this one; I guess I shouldn't leave it lying around. I grab that, and the plastic first aid suitcase that's stored in the cheap overhead baggage compartment.

I make my way back to the kitchen, once inside the house. There's four of the kids lying head-to-toe on the two couches. They seem to be sleeping. I wonder what they've seen of what happened tonight; what they understand, what they believe. They really didn't need more stuff to have nightmares about. But I can't worry about that now.

Luke's cleaning the blood away from Lori's skin when I come in. She looks a lot cleaner, though her shirt is still full of blood; she took off her coat, I don't know when or where. I put our modern first aid kit on the counter next to Erik's antique, and Lori looks at me. She looks calmer, now, like she's regaining a bit of her attitude. It makes me feel better. She's supposed to be bossy and obnoxious, and that's how I like her. I can't describe the feeling it gives me to see her scared and helpless.

There's a knock at the door that has me jumping and reaching for the gun I no longer have, and I share an intense look with Luke and Erik before I remember the pastrami I ordered. The guy starts arguing when I give him a hundred dollar bill, but he shuts up when I tell him to keep the change. I guess next time I make an emergency stash, I'll make sure to keep half of it in twenties.

There's whimpering in the kitchen when I get back; Luke is sewing up Lori's neck, and she's crying. I almost don't walk in when I see it. I've never been good with girls, especially when they're crying. But Erik's noticed me, so I can't walk away now without needing to explain. Instead, I focus on him so I don't have to look at Lori, and I show the brown paper bag in my hands.

"Pastrami sandwiches for everybody."

Luke keeps squinting at his work through his glasses, but I hear the relief in his voice, despite his expression.

"Good! I'm starving. And they'll do Lori and you a world of good." He turns to Erik. "Got any orange juice?"

"I got beer. And water."

"Water it is."

Lori has a little smile, a ghost of the expression she uses when she wants to seduce guys into giving her stuff.

"Well, actually, I could use a beer..."

"No alcohol for you until this starts to scab."

She sighs, but she knows as well as I do that when our health is concerned, what Luke says goes. Erik goes to a cupboard and pulls out two mugs. He rinses them before filling them with tap water, and hands one to Lori. When he goes to give me the other, I wave a hand to refuse, showing him the two-liter plastic bottle in my other hand.

"Got me some coke."

Luke cuts off the string and reaches for a cloth to clean her neck with.

"That's ok, but you should still drink some water."

"Don't forget I made you coffee."

"It's all good. I'm not planning to go to bed. I have to be out of here pretty early in the morning anyway."

"Yeah, you really do."

Erik doesn't look at me, but I know a veiled threat when I hear one.

"I'll leave when I damn want. Keep being a good host and everything will be fine."

He looks at me and chuckles. I'm inches away from punching him. No one laughs when I threaten them. But when he opens his mouth and speaks, I know I've won, so I don't push it any further.

"Fine, fine. You can stay as long as you want. But don't expect me to spend any money. And keep them out of my fridge."

AUGUST 31ST, 4:57 AM

Erik's shower is pretty weird. It's in an old-fashioned tub with feet and a curtain that wraps all around it, but the showerhead is wide, and the water is hot. I have to wash my hair and body with a bar of soap and a washcloth, 'cause he doesn't own anything else. It takes a hell of a long time to get all the blood out of my hair with that, though, and the water's getting cold by the time I'm done. At least, he's got towels. And a mirror.

It's good I don't really need a shave, 'cause he doesn't seem to have any razors, either. The cuts on my face and scalp are healing nicely. I took off the butterfly closures yesterday. I have a big black and purple bruise all over the left side of my face, though. I tie my hair and pick up Erik's clothes to put them on again. I'm going to have to ask Jimmy to bring me something to wear. He's roughly the same size as I am, and Erik's clothes really suck.

I yawn and wipe my eyes again. I'm more tired than I should be after spending the night up; after all, I slept the whole day before. I check the bite mark on my neck. It's ugly, but less so than the one on my arm. It seems to be healing all right; I wrap it in gauze more to hide it than to protect it.

I pick up my new phone before I go, and the empty silver cigarette case. I smoked every cigarette I had while waiting up with Lori, Luke and Erik. I came to take a shower as much because I needed it as to take my mind off being out.

When I get downstairs, Lori and Luke are lying on the floor with some pillows and blankets. I can't see Erik, so I get to the kitchen. He's there all right, and so is a brand new pack of cigarettes, still wrapped in plastic and everything. He's boiling some water, and I can see the French press has been cleaned, and there's some ground coffee at the bottom of it.

"Had a good shower?"

"Yeah. Where'd you find the cigarettes?"

"I went to the corner store. There's one open all night right on the corner of the street."

I pick it up. It's not my brand, but they're decent, and he went through the trouble.

"Thanks for going to get them."

"No problem. To tell you the truth, I wasn't sure I could handle you when you're not smoking. You're a tense guy."

I hold back the urge to snap at him; after all, that would only prove his point. I tear off the plastic packaging, and light a cigarette before putting the rest of them into the silver case. His kettle screams, and he pours the water into the press.

"So, what are you going to do now?"

I wonder what his angle is. Does he want to know what I'll do about the vampires, or does he simply want me and the kids out?

"About what?"

"In general."

He's asking about the vampires. He's not been afraid to be specific about the kids before, there's no reason he should be now.

"I'm going to get some more information about these things. So I can find them and fight them."

"Oh?"

He raises his eyebrows at me as he presses the filter of the French press down. He looks amused, so I keep my tone and my words conversational.

"Yeah. I'm thinking if I ask the right guy, I might get some answers."

"The right guy, huh?"

He's smiling, but he's not looking at me. He's catching on. He goes to the cupboard to grab a mug from it.

"Yeah... someone who knows intimately about them, who knows who they are and where they live... you know, someone involved."

He grins at me as he pours the coffee in the mug. This time, it's in the shape of Darth Vader's head. He slides it over to me before he answers.

"And where do you think you'll find that?"

"Well, you're a vampire. I figured I'd ask you."

Again, he doesn't deny it. He just shrugs and takes a comfortable seat next to me at the counter.

"And what makes you think I'll say anything?"

I shrug. I'm not usually that good at double-talk and all that messed up subtle shit Lupino does. But it seems to me this guy is making it easy for me. Maybe he wants to tell. That'd make my life easier, anyhow.

"'Cause you don't want me involved, and they're coming after me, so if you want me to stay alive and not be turned into one of theirs like you said, you're gonna have to help me out."

"I am, am I?"

"You are if there's any truth to what you said before. You know, about not being on their side, and not wanting to let them have me... if you want me on your side, you're gonna be up front with me. 'Cause they put my kids in danger now. There's no way I'm letting this go. I'm going after them, with or without you."

He leans his head in his hand, smiling at me. He stays silent for a while. I guess he's making up his mind; I don't want to add anything, in case I change it to my disadvantage, so I start drinking some coffee. It's too hot, and even though I can't feel the burn, it doesn't taste like anything, so I put it down and light another cigarette. He watches me with his stupid smirk all the while, so I don't know if he's even really hesitating or if he's just making me sweat.

"I guess you have a point. So, what do you want to know?"

"How many are there?"

"Hard to tell. They're expanding. When I last checked, there were only about a dozen or so, but I guess it could have doubled or even tripled by now."

"What do they want?"

He makes a face. It's the first time I get the impression he's serious about anything.

"To piss me off."

I raise my eyebrows. Am I supposed to believe that? He takes a look at me and starts laughing. I don't think it's that funny.

"Don't look so shocked. Vampires can be pretty petty."

"So their sole purpose is to piss you off?"

He shrugs and seems to consider it. If he's serious, he's either a force to be reckoned with, or just some asshole who's really full of himself. At this point, I would believe both.

"Well. Maybe not their sole purpose. But certainly at least their number two goal. If it wasn't, they would never have come here."

"Why?"

He pauses, but he's not looking at me, so I think he's gathering his thoughts rather than holding out, and I drink my coffee to help me stay quiet. It's not so hot anymore, but now it just tastes like crap, like I let it sit too long. He sighs and relaxes back into his chair, and he still doesn't look at me as he talks.

"This is my town. I've never allowed groups to form here, and they know that full well, and did before they came. The fact that they're trying to settle here has to be to spite me, somehow."

This doesn't make any sense. Why now? Why not before? Why him? Why doesn't he do anything, if he can?

"Why?"

"Well, their leader is notoriously bold. He got pretty hot in Europe some time ago. Tried the same scheme, wiped out a huge, ancient gang that had been established there for centuries. Last I heard, they were happily settled there. Now, here they are. I haven't found out what happened yet."

"And why do you think they're specifically out to piss you off?"

He makes a face and avoids my eyes; he's going to give me a non-answer again.

"Let's just say I have a reputation with their type."

"Right. Whatever that means."

He nods once, a bit noncommittally, as if to let me know he's not going to say any more on the subject. I sigh and light another cigarette. I pick up the mug to drink from it, but I have to put it back down 'cause I'm out of coffee. I take out my phone and check the time. It's nearly five thirty, so I decide to try Jimmy's phone. I'll need a couple of tries to wake him up at this hour, unless he hasn't gone to bed yet. I get voice mail, but I don't leave a message. I'll call back in a couple minutes.

"Ok, so they're out to piss you off. Why haven't they killed you yet?"

He chuckles, reaches for the French press, and pours the rest of the coffee in my mug.

"How would they be able to piss me off if I was dead?"

"All right, so what's their game, then?"

He puts down the press and shrugs.

"Actually, it's a little hard to tell. I thought they were mainly after me, but then they started coming after the remains of the Russian gangs. Then I thought they were after you, but they didn't come after you direct. And they were kind of sloppy fighting you, too."

"They did come after me."

"Well, sort of."

"What do you mean, sort of? We barely got out of there!"

"I'm sure you barely got out of there because you were protecting people. Tell me, how did they get in?"

"Lori invited them in. Why?"

"That's your girlfriend, right?"

I have to fight the urge to punch the asshole. What's his problem, anyway?

"She's not my girlfriend. Not that it's any of your business."

"Anyway. Why did she invite them in? Is it her habit to invite strangers to come into her home?"

"Well, no... she knew one of the guys. That's how I knew something was wrong, actually."

"Why?"

"The guy was one of mine. I sent him after Bogdan and his gang. I figured he was killed, 'cause I didn't hear from him for days afterwards. When he showed up, I knew he must be one of these bastards."

"See, this is exactly what I mean."

"What?"

"Well, if you knew the guy, and they were after you, they would have sent him to you directly. And they wouldn't have waited until you were sure to know what he was, either. More likely, they just wanted to talk. About what is anyone's guess."

He does make a pretty good point. I suppose I would have seen it sooner or later, but with all the excitement, I haven't had time to think. He watches me put the dots together in my mind with that annoying knowing expression. It makes me wanna go on saying stuff, even though I haven't finished thinking it through.

"So if it's not you, and it's not me, who are they after?"

"That is the question. Who, or what."

"And you're gonna tell me you don't know?"

"I'm not sure."

"But you have an idea."

"Actually..."

"You got nothing?"

He shrugs, grinning guilelessly.

"It's hard to tell. They're not moving like I expect them to. For example, I thought for sure they'd go after one of the big groups, like the O'Reily's or the Lupino group. When they settled in the Russian district, I thought they were just biding their time, but then they started taking over your strip joints. They could, and should, have taken over the whole operation by now. I mean, no offense, kid, but your operation isn't the biggest or most tightly run in town."

I shrug. There's no offense to be taken there; I'm trying to keep our heads out of the water, not put together the next big family.

"Tell me something I don't know. So?"

"So, why are they beating around the bush? Why not attack you before? Why send a guy to talk to you, instead of just ambushing you somewhere? If they're trying to take over the town by taking over your group, they're going at it the wrong way."

"And you think that's what they're up to?"

"It would fit their M.O."

"You know what their M.O. is?"

"I told you, I've heard of them before. Anyway, usually they prey on the homeless and the weak until they've got safety in numbers. Then they start going after the lower ranks of the biggest power in town, working their way up, turning them, until they reach the top. Then all there's left to do is turn the leader and they've got the city."

I drink the coffee he poured me. I need time to analyze all this. Did he say turn? And does that mean what I think it does?

I glance at the microwave oven to read the time, but it's a really old model, one that works with a dial and not a trace of anything digital in sight. I take out my cell phone. It's a quarter to six, so I try Jimmy again. No luck. It gives me time to formulate a question, at least.

"So, when you say turn, you mean, made into a vampire, right?"

"Yes."

"So, how would making important people into vampires help them control a city?"

He leans his head in his hand to look at me, like he's watching a chimp and is deciding whether or not it's worth his time talking to it. His eyes are dark; I imagine his skin must have been pretty dark at some point, too, but now it's pale. It makes him look like a cancer patient. He seems to be thinking. I light another cigarette to give him time to make up his mind about whatever it is he wants to say.

"When a vampire is made, they owe a sort of... loyalty to the one that made them."

This statement raises too many questions at once for me to pick the best one to ask, so I let him go on. He's searching his mind, like he's explaining something difficult to put in words. It doesn't seem so much emotional as complicated.

"Well... it's a bit like magic. When a vampire makes another one, they have a measure of control over them."

"Control how?"

"Well, it's a willpower thing. Usually, the elder vampire can tell the younger one what to do, and the younger one has to do it. And the younger one can't go against his creator, stuff like that."

This is starting to make a weird, fucked up kind of sense, but I can't decide how yet.

"Ok. So they turn these important guys, and they control them, so they control the city. If they were successful before, why not stop then? Why start over somewhere else?"

"Well, when vampires get old enough, they get more power-ful. Tougher to kill, more resistant, stuff like that. Their willpower is also stronger."

"So, what, they don't have to obey anymore?"

"Something like that."

"So they lose control of the city. I get it. How long's it take, usually?"

"It depends on the strength of mind of the vampire that was turned. It can take centuries, for some, or only decades, even years, for others."

I watch him. He was so guarded with me a couple days ago, when I woke up in his living room. He wasn't even willing to admit to being a vampire then, and now he's telling me all sorts of trade secrets. I don't know what it is that's making him tell me the truth now, but there has to be something. It might be because those other fucks attacked me, and he feels responsible. Or maybe he thinks I'm forced to help him. Or it might just be that I'm leaving all my kids in his home and he has the power to kill them all as soon as I turn my back on him. I guess circumstances like that are pretty good to build trust on. I decide to get bolder.

"So, how many vampires have you made?"

He has a sort of dry chuckle towards me, showing me his teeth rather than smiling. I know he's got it in him to kill all of them; there's no question about that. I've seen that kind of look before. I shouldn't have brought them here; I've put them all in danger. What was I thinking?

"Real subtle, kid. I'm different.'

"What, 'cause you're just a dark tortured creature who has a hard time reconciling with his nature? 'Cause deep down, you're just misunderstood?"

He stares at me with wide eyes for like five seconds and then he bursts out laughing. He laughs and laughs, slaps his thighs, and wipes his eyes. He does it loud, and long, without ever even drawing any breath. Eventually, he ends up doubled over and silent, like he doesn't have enough air to make a sound and his hilarity is too great for him to breathe in. It lasts long enough for me to feel like the joke's on me, and then for me to see how funny that can be. I mean, that guy looks like an Emo hipster, not an evil mastermind.

He eventually calms down by the time I'm laughing too, and he wipes his eyes, taking a deep breath.

"You're a riot. But don't delude yourself: all that shit you see on TV and in the pictures is just that, shit. I don't know a single vampire I could describe as tortured. Misunderstood, that, for sure. Vampires are monsters, and incapable of feeling any sort of remorse whatsoever, and they're not conflicted about their food. I mean, I understand the morbid fascination, but whatever happened to running in fear in front of predators?"

"So why should I trust anything you say, then?"

"It's all about enlightened self-interest, if you ask me. You need me."

"And what about you? Do you need me? Why haven't you killed me yet?"

He smiles at me, and I see the twinkle in his eyes. He thinks this is funny. I bet it is, for him. Just a game he plays.

"Should I?"

"Well, wouldn't you have better control over me if you made me like you?"

He has that amused expression. His smile is coy.

"Like me?"

Asshole. Does he seriously think he can still pretend he's just a normal regular human?

"Really? You're gonna keep fucking with me at this point? After everything you told me?"

He chuckles, and shakes his head.

"That's a hell of a temper. Relax. I'm different because I'm bored with this crap. You get to be my age, you'll crave any kind of entertainment. So I try to take people as they are. It's more interesting that way. But if you're worried about yourself, or the kids, don't. I got more interesting things to do."

I watch him, but I don't answer. His argument's not too strong, but I think he's telling the truth. He's made a point of avoiding every question that bothered him so far. Why would he start lying now? I light another cigarette so I can think, but I can't come up with another good question. Except for one.

"So, how old are you?"

He snorts, and laughs, then looks down at my empty cup of coffee.

"Want more coffee? I think there's some left in the freezer."

I sigh. Of course, it wasn't going to be that easy.

"Nah, I'm fine. Besides, I gotta go soon."

If it wasn't Lupino, I would have canceled so I could stay here with the kids. I can at least have Jimmy drive me and then come back here right away. That makes me think. I pick up the phone again and hit the green button twice, calling Jimmy. He's still not picking up, but it's starting to be more urgent, so I call him again right away. This time, he answers.

"What the fuck do you want?"

"It's Alex. I need a ride."

"I know it's you, man, but seriously, have you seen the time? Who the hell is up at this hour anyways?"

"I am, obviously. I gotta go eat breakfast with Lupino. Get out of bed and come pick me up now."

"Whatever. I'm on my way."

"You have to come pick me up on Walker Street again, at 337. Remember where it is?"

"The hell are you doing there?"

"It's actually kind of a long story. Can you bring me your best suit, too? I promise I'll give it back when I'm done, but right now I have nothing to wear."

"Don't you want me to swing by your place and pick one up for you?"

"No. The house burned down. That's a long story too. Just get here and I'll explain in the car."

"... fine. But I better have an Irish coffee waiting for me there."

I hang up and look at Erik. He's been cleaning out the coffee maker and the mug. He doesn't seem to have a dishwasher.

"Do you know how to make an Irish coffee?"

AUGUST 31ST, 7:03 AM

I wait for Jimmy on the front steps. The sun is rising, and Erik is still in the kitchen, but I needed to be alone a few minutes. I'm already halfway through the pack he bought me a couple hours ago, but it's ok, I can buy more.

I see Jimmy start to pull into the driveway, but the bus is blocking the way, so he backs up and parks in the street instead. He still looks a bit pissed when I see him walk up to me, but mostly he seems confused and a little alarmed. He's holding a Wawa plastic bag, and he gestures towards me with his chin.

"What the fuck happened last night, boss?"

"We were attacked. Mark came back, with a couple of those monsters."

"Why didn't you call me?'

"Happened kinda fast. It was over in less time than it would have taken to dial."

He gives a small glance towards the bus, and then holds out his hand, gesturing quickly with his fingers, so I take out my smokes and hand him one. He gets out his Zippo and lights it, taking the time to take two drags before speaking.

"So... is everyone all right?"

He doesn't look at me as he says it. He likes everyone to think he's a heartless bastard, but I know there's stuff he cares about. He might have been out already by the time I took over the brothel and freed the kids, but he still cared about the ones left inside, in his own way.

"They're all fine. Lori got a little hurt, but she'll be ok."

He nods, and quickly looks around for something else to talk about, so I can forget this little lapse of emotion.

"I got you my best suit like you asked, but I ain't sure you're gonna like it."

He hands me the Wawa bag, and I peer inside. It's not the cleanest I've ever seen, and it's black, but it'll do. I imagined all sorts of horrible things like brown corduroy or green plaid, so I'm pretty happy, even though I might look like I'm attending a funeral.

"Great. Thanks. Come on in, I got your coffee. And don't make too much noise, they're all asleep inside."

He frowns uncertainly up at the house.

"Why'd you bring them here? I mean, you told me you didn't trust this guy."

I glare at him. Sometimes, he can be so dense.

"Where else was I gonna go? Would you prefer I had brought them to your place? I'll take them to a hotel later, but I gotta get them some clothes first so they don't look like a bunch of refugees."

He nods once, and steps inside. I know he trusts my judgment, but I had to rely heavily on his advice when I started out, and he always questions what I do, at least a little, to make sure I have all the facts straight. It works.

I follow him inside. Luke, Lori and the other four eldest ones are still asleep in the living room, though I'm sure they'll be getting up soon. I'm extra careful not to make a sound so I don't bother them, and I follow Jimmy to the kitchen. I'm gonna change there, just in case they get at each other's throats. I don't think I need to worry about Erik. If he wanted blood, he would have had it by now, but Jimmy's a bit more volatile.

Erik's sitting at the island counter. He's gotten a few of his books out of the living room shelves while I was waiting outside, and now he's leafing through them. I don't know how he did it without waking anyone up, but I've seen he can be really quiet when he wants. There's a cup of coffee and a bottle of whiskey on the counter, too. Jimmy and him look at each other for a while. I know Jimmy's starting a staring contest, and he's trying to get Erik to back off. Erik holds his stare for a few seconds, and then seems to start to think it's funny. I've not known a lot of people who knew who Jimmy was and could still smile in his presence. But Erik grins and breaks eye contact with him to gesture to the bottle and mug on the counter.

"Hey. Hear you like a good Irish coffee. Check it out."

Jimmy looks at him suspiciously for a little while more, and then finally looks down at the bottle, as if to humor him. But the bottle obviously catches his eye, and he picks it up, whistling through his teeth. He admires it a bit before raising an eyebrow at Erik.

"Bushmills 16 year-old single malt?"

Erik shrugs amiably, putting his book down on top of the others. All three are open and lying on their spine.

"It's all I got."

"Fine."

He turns the bottle over in his hands. I can relax now; he's fascinated, and it doesn't matter what Erik is anymore. I put down the bag and start changing. Jimmy might be fine now, but I'm neither crazy nor stupid. He picks up the coffee mug, and sniffs its contents like it's full of dog shit, then goes to pour it out in the sink. Erik smirks and he raises his eyebrow.

"Not in the mood for coffee anymore?"

"Mix this with coffee? Are you nuts? Gimme some ice."

He rinses out the mug carefully while Erik goes to his freezer. I can see the freezer is also empty save for a bag of ice and a can of coffee. He takes out the bag and tosses it to Jimmy.

"Here. Have fun. It's a little stuck, and I don't have an ice pick."

Jimmy catches the bag, and hits it on the counter a couple of times to break the ice, then throws a few bits in a glass and pours in the whiskey. I know he drinks in the morning sometimes, but I thought he had enough respect for me not to do it in my face. I try to hold back the urge I have to throw the bottle against the wall. It's his business if he wants to get drunk, and he's never hit anyone that didn't deserve it at least a little when he was in that state, but it doesn't mean I have to like it.

"I'll wait in the car."

I turn around, not waiting for his reaction, and walk out of the kitchen. Luke is still asleep, and I don't have the heart to wake him, so I just go to the bag to grab a thousand bucks or so out of it, and put it in the inner pocket of the black suit I'm wearing. I might stop and pick up a few things for the kids. I see Lori stirring in her sleep, and I'm afraid she might wake up, so I go out to wait in the car like I said. It'll take the time it takes, 'cause I'm not going back in. I hate watching people drink.

AUGUST 31ST, 7:56 AM

Jimmy drives away as quickly as he can when he drops me off in front of Lupino's house. It took him forever to come out of Erik's house, and all he's wanted to do since then is get back in. I try to tell myself it's just the whiskey he loves, but I think he might actually be getting along with Erik. It's not like I care, though. I just like to have him around while the kids are there. Not that I don't believe Erik when he says he won't hurt them, but I like to know someone can make sure he doesn't.

I ring the doorbell, and look at my reflection in the window as I wait for an answer to come. I look as good as I'm going to. The door flies open and Rosanna is suddenly filling it, grinning at me. She grabs my face in both her hands and kisses my cheeks, then pushes me away, holding my shoulders, to look me up and down.

"Look at that face! Did you get in more trouble, Alex? You should be more careful. Come in, come in! We've been waiting!"

She leads me inside, and gestures to the small living room before heading towards the kitchen. I head over there, and see Lupino replacing a book on a shelf. He's dressed and showered. I wonder how long he's been waiting for me. As he turns to greet me, though, I can see the expression on his face is still friendly, but very serious.

"Alex, my boy, more injuries? And what is this I hear about your house burning down?"

I try to contain my surprise. I should have known he would know. He always seems to know everything.

"Well, it's kind of a long and complicated story."

"We have time to talk. Rosanna is making us breakfast as we speak. I do believe events have gone beyond superficial explanations."

I nod. He's right. At this point, he can't ignore it, and I have to tell him the truth, or as much of it as I can. I try to look around for a way to bring up the subject. My eyes fall on the picture above the fireplace, and something primal stirs in my mind. That face... All thoughts of explanations get mixed up in all the rest of the jumble in my head. It takes Lupino touching my arm to bring me out of it, and when I look down at him, he's not even smiling anymore.

"Alex? What is it?"

I clear my throat. There's no way I can say what's on my mind without sounding crazy or at least incredibly offensive.

"Um, maybe we could discuss it over breakfast?"

He nods. He won't stare at me like Luke would, but he gives me a small look that tells me he's trying to work out what's wrong with me. At least, I bought myself a couple of minutes; it's not polite or good to bring up business inside the house, anyway. This isn't business, strictly speaking, but he doesn't know that yet.

Instead of the dining room, he brings me through the back door to the garden. It's a cozy kind of place, enclosed in a brick wall on all four sides, with all sorts of plants all over. There's a couple of statues, and a white stone bench at the bottom. Right at the entrance, though, inside a little open solarium that separates the house from the garden, is a little stone terrace with a small metal and glass patio set in the middle. This is the place where I first met him, two years ago, though it seems like much longer than that. I can see the brown spot on the stones where I bled, though it's almost gone. He moved the table; it used to be right over it.

He sits slowly, watching me. I catch myself and walk to join him, but not before he notices what I was looking at.

"I have breakfast here every day, weather permitting. Ever since that day. It was a happy day for me. I like to be reminded of it."

"Yeah. It was a good day."

He nods and watches me sit. It wasn't a happy day for me, not exactly, though in retrospect, its outcome was very good. It was the most difficult part of my takeover, only months after I had unwittingly seized control of what used to be the Borodinski group. My own guys were at each other's throats as often as they were trying to kill me. One of them, Nick, had actually won my trust, but ended up betraying me for the Chinese, and shooting me in an attempt to take over only a couple of days after Jack showed up at my place with Lupino's offer. I finally realized then I couldn't manage this on my weight alone, and I had to join up with one of the larger organizations. So I patched up my gunshot wound as best I could, and broke into Lupino's backyard so I could talk to him direct and set my terms. He had been having breakfast back then, too.

Rosanna comes in holding a tray with a teapot and two china cups. I don't notice her until she's right next to me, but I do before she puts the cups down, so at least I don't look like an idiot. She pours us some coffee from the teapot and leaves it on the table, along with a creamer, but no sugar. I guess she knows I take mine black.

Lupino thanks her and pours a bit of cream in his cup, mixing it in with a spoon. He waits for her to walk away before he looks up at me. He looks at the bandages on my neck, the bruises on my face, and Jimmy's suit, which is slightly rumpled, the wrong color, and not entirely the right fit. He's not noticing, though; he's pointing with his eyes, letting me know he's seen everything and now he wants explanations. He doesn't like to have to ask. I sigh. I don't know how to say what I have to say. I know that the word vampire should probably not cross my lips; I don't want him to think I'm unstable, or nuts.

"You were right. The problem I'm having... is a little more serious than I let on at first."

He's watching me with a serious expression, the lines between his eyebrows made deeper and more apparent by his frown. I put my hands together and lean forward to give me a few seconds to think about my next sentence. I have to somehow make him understand that this is something personal, and it won't affect the business or the family. It'd be nice if he thought I was still in control, though that's not the entire truth anymore. I wait too long.

"And why did you not keep me informed as I asked?"

He's pissed. Another might have missed it; not me, though. I know him too well. I can see the tightness around his mouth.

"Well, it's a bit complicated... also, it doesn't really concern the family. Or the business."

That doesn't make him happy; he's got that neutral face he has when people are giving him bad news.

"What is it about, then?"

"Well, I'm not sure yet. But I think it was a fluke that it touched one of our groups."

I wait for his reaction. There is none, of course; at least, none that I can read. He keeps staring at me with that careful neutral expression he has when he's displeased. It's unreasonable how uneasy he can make me feel with just a look; no one ever made me feel like that, not Mikov's bastards, not even the man my mother made me with. His tone is flat, and a bit sarcastic.

"A fluke that burned down your house and injured you to this extent."

He glances at my neck again, but not pointedly. In fact, the motion is so slight that I have trouble catching it at all, and I'm suddenly sure he didn't intend for me to see it. I don't know what it means, but I'm sure it means something. He doesn't ever do anything for nothing. Besides, the bruises on my face are far more spectacular than the bandages on my neck. I have to weigh my words carefully.

"Well... it affected one of my biggest earners, so I stuck my nose in it. It's just become... personal, that's all. Nothing to do with us. Well, you."

The look he gives me is at least mildly annoyed; I think I can see him glancing at my neck again. He opens his mouth to speak, but he turns towards the door when we both hear Rosanna's distinctive humming. I lift my head to see her come in with a tray full of freshly baked brioches, and three small mason jars full of different sorts of jam. She sets the tray down on the table. I can smell the brioches; I didn't realize I was this hungry. Now I have to fight back the urge to grab three and stuff them in my mouth all at once. I manage to wait until Lupino's thanked her and taken one for himself before I grab two and eat half of one in one bite. I hardly chew, swallow, and inhale the rest of it before he has time to break his open and think about what kind of jam he wants. I see that his humor has improved, though; he's smiling now, looking at me like I'm doing something really funny. I swallow and look away; I hope I'm not doing something as stupid and wussy as blushing, but I think I can feel my cheeks warm. He pretends he doesn't notice, though I know he does, and spreads some raspberry jam on his brioche.

I wait to pick up the next one until he's eaten at least half of his, though it's surprisingly hard. He picks up the conversation right where we left it, not even looking at me, keeping his eyes on his knife as he spreads jam on the second half of his brioche.

"If I understand you correctly, you think that a matter which robs you of one of your biggest earners and your own home, on top of nearly killing you more than once is not something that should concern me or our family?"

I have to look down, and this time I do blush. Put like that, it does sound like I'm an idiot who doesn't know his dick from his elbow. But what else can I say? The truth? I look up into his eyes. It is what he wants, but how can I give it to him? How will he believe it? I start eating my second brioche without putting jam on it to give me more time to think about the way I'm going to phrase this.

"It's... a little more complex than that. And it's very hard to explain."

He takes a drink from his coffee, and then dips his brioche in it. He chews on a piece of it as he speaks. He's so casual, he could be talking about the weather.

"We have all the time we need for long and complex explanations. Please go ahead."

I sip my coffee before I start. There is really only one more way I can try not to say it.

"Well... as you know, I'm not exactly human."

He nods, but he feels the need to correct me about it again. He doesn't like it when I say that.

"You have abilities which most men do not."

"Right. Well, anyway... this is business that concerns... people like me."

He puts his cup down and stares at the bandage on my neck. There's nothing hidden, or subtle about it; he's pointing it out.

"I think that has to be a simplification."

That's it; he's going to make me say it. I sigh and I touch the spot on my neck where the mark is of when that thing bit me. That vampire that looked so... holy shit.

My eyes focus on Mister Lupino and I see that he's noticed my expression; I've never seen perplexity so plain on his face before.

"What is it, Alex?"

"Mister Lupino... sir... that picture of your family hanging in your living room..."

He frowns and his expression becomes serious, intent, even.

"What about it?"

"Could I... go take another look at it?"

He stares at me while he finishes chewing the remainder of his bite, then wipes his mouth and hands with his napkin and reaches into one of his pant pockets. He retrieves a brown leather wallet, and opens it to start searching for something inside. I wipe my hands too; he's probably going to hand me something. He takes out a small, faded picture from one of the folds and looks at it forlornly for just a moment before giving it to me. I feel a chill when I look down at it. There's no young Lupino in this picture, and no wife either; just the son. How did he know that was what I wanted to see?

I turn it over in my hands, like the back is going to reveal something hidden. It's slightly yellowed, and the corners are rounded by age. It's not like I really think there's going to be answers there, but I don't know what else to do at this point. I turn the picture over to look at the front again. He looks a bit younger in the picture, and the personality is completely different; he's laughing, his eyes turning up and sparkling just like his father's do when he smiles, but there's no mistake to be made. This is definitely the vampire that kicked my ass at the Exxxotic. What can I possibly tell him? He thinks his son is dead. He's right, but not as much as he thinks he is, I guess. As I give him back the picture, the look Lupino gives me is more intense than any I've ever seen on his face before. Looks like I'm going to have to break my rule about asking personal questions. Shit, I wish I could smoke in front of him right now.

"Your son... I don't know how to ask you this, but... well..."

I take a deep breath. I fucking hate having to tiptoe like this.

"Your son. How did he... what happened to him?"

He takes back the picture without looking at it; he just stares at me with an expression I've never seen before. He doesn't look pissed off, exactly, though it's pretty close to it. After a few interminable minutes of silence, he looks down at the picture and his features soften a bit. He's still silent. There are three brioches left. They smell delicious, and I'm still starving, but I know my throat is way too tight to swallow anything right now. He finally puts the picture back, sighing, and he picks up his cup of coffee to sip it thoughtfully, still not looking at me. His eyes finally meet mine when he's ready to speak. I think they're glistening; is he holding back tears?

"He was killed, along with my wife. Or rather it is assumed. He was not... found."

He takes another sip of coffee and puts the cup down. I say nothing. I don't have much experience in personal matters, and I don't want to say something wrong, so I let him think about what he wants to say.

"Why do you ask? Does it have to do with the matter at hand?"

He looks pained, and annoyed. I wish he'd give me something more to go on. I hate to prod, and I can't possibly tell him what's on my mind, either, but now I gotta answer his question.

"How? I mean... if it's not too indiscreet... how were they...?"

He looks at my neck again, quickly, before picking up his cup of coffee. I don't think I'm supposed to notice, but I can't help it. Does he know what I have to tell him? How can I use that to my advantage?

After stirring his coffee with a spoon for a while, he looks up at me and points at his own neck.

"What happened to your neck?"

I decide to take off the bandage to show him. If I'm right, he'll have seen this before, and it'll be the only way that either of us will take the first step. I do it slow, because I'm kind of dreading the moment I'll have it off. What if it means nothing? Then I'll have to use diplomacy. I hate diplomacy.

His eyes widen as he stares at the bite mark on my neck. I've seen it, so I know it's neater and a lot less mangled than the one on my arm, but if you know what you're looking at, it is definitely the scarier of the two. He leans forward to examine it, and then nods gravely.

"I see. How exactly did you know that your business is the same as the one that took my wife and child?"

I stare at him, but catch myself after a few seconds and start re-wrapping my neck. So, it seems he won't think I'm so crazy after all.

"Well... I wasn't sure. But I did want to be sure you wouldn't think I'm crazy."

He has a small smile, but it doesn't touch his eyes.

"Alex, my boy, with the things that you can do, there are a lot of things that would no longer come as a surprise."

I guess he's got a point there. I nod. My hand goes to the cigarette case in my pocket, but I leave it there. I know I can't smoke in front of him, but damn if I don't really need a cigarette right now. I sigh. At least, the stressful part is over, now that I know he's inclined to believe me.

"I honestly think I'm the best person to handle this matter. My power is the only thing that's kept me alive and above the water all this time."

He nods, and sighs heavily. His face is full of wrinkles, and his hair is white, but this is the first time I really think he looks old. He takes another sip of his coffee and sets his cup back down on the table.

"Alex. About my family..."

He looks up at me, and I can see pain again in his eyes, with just a hint of despair. It almost hurts to see it. I wish I could give him the peace he needs, but all I have is bad news, and I can't bring myself to say it. I look down at my cup of coffee, wishing to hell I could light a cigarette already. He waits for me to speak, but I don't. I won't say it. I can't stand the look in his eyes now; I can't imagine what it would be if he knew the truth of it.

"Alex, if you know anything, you must speak up. Do not leave an old man in doubt. Is my son involved in what is going on?"

I look him in the eye. His worry is as evident as his pain. I can't lie to him, and I can't tell him the truth. It's fortunate that I don't really have to do either of those things. After all, that thing can't be his son anymore. Can it?

"No. He's not."

He looks slightly relieved, but not enough for me to be sure he believes me. I guess he understands what I'm saying, at least. He reaches for another brioche and breaks it open, but there's no enthusiasm to his gestures. I look at the food, but I don't even feel hungry anymore. It's not just my throat that feels tight anymore; my whole stomach's in knots. He refills his coffee using the pot Rosanna left on the table, and pours cream in it.

"Tell me, Alex, what has become of your young charges now that your house has burned down?"

The kids. I had almost forgotten about them. I nearly take out my phone to look at the time, but then I realize how rude that would be, and I leave it in my pocket.

"They're staying with a friend for now. I'm going to put them up at a hotel later, though."

He nods a bit. He seems to be regaining a little of his good humor, if slowly.

"You do not like to impose, do you."

I shake my head; he should know that by now. I like to stand on my own two feet. When you let others support you, all you're really asking for is for them to throw you to the ground. His smile almost reaches his eyes. I can see a little bit of the pride he shows when I do something that makes him happy.

"Were any of them hurt in the incident?"

"No."

"Good. Is it the first time someone comes after you in your own home?"

"Yeah. Most of the guys that have double-crossed me so far have at least had the good taste to do it when I was out on business."

I know what he's saying, but I don't feel like I have to acknowledge it. Yeah, it was probably stupid and reckless of me not to move out sooner, but I'm still learning here.

"So, then, have you given more consideration to the offer I made on your birthday?"

He's casual again, looking at his brioche while he's spreading jam on it, but I know he only acts like that when the answer really matters. I'm surprised, though. After what just happened, I didn't think he'd be keen to have me under his roof. He seems to be waiting for me to go on, so I say what's on my mind.

"I... didn't think you would want that kind of a risk."

His smile does reach his eyes, this time.

"Are you worried about my safety?"

I'm about to say yes, but I suddenly realize how ridiculous that sounds, and I can't help but chuckle. It must be the fatigue.

"As you most certainly realize, my position brings with it many threats. Like I said before, having you here would be much more of a deterrent than it would be an invitation for trouble."

I calm down, and try to be serious. My head is spinning, so I finish my coffee before I answer.

"Actually, I have thought about it, Mister Lupino. I would be honored to come live here with you."

His face warms up and he leans over to tap my arm, gently.

"Good, good. I will have Rosanna prepare your room."

AUGUST 31ST, 12:31 PM

It's too bad I don't have time to get some respectable tailor-made suits, but at least I can have them made in under a week and walk out with a couple of decent ready-to-wears. I put one on before I leave the tailor's and put the other one in a bag so I can bring it to a bus station and leave it in a locker for emergency access. I have the taxi wait for me at every stop.

I get to a large surface and pick up a couple more prepaid phones so I can give one to Luke and keep the other; I'm almost out of time on the one I'm using now, but there's enough to give a couple calls still. I use it to call Erik while I pick out a bunch of identical t-shirts and shorts for the kids, along with underwear and socks. They'll probably not be the right size, but at least it'll be something for them to wear. The phone rings forever, and I'm about to hang up when Erik finally picks up.

"Yeah?"

"It's Alex. Put Luke on the phone."

"You know, kid, you could use a few more manners. You'd get along a lot better with lots more people if you tried using honey to attract flies, you know what I'm saying?"

"What are you now, my mother? Just put Luke on the phone."

The bastard laughs, but I hear him call for Luke. There are a few muffled sounds, but then Luke picks up the phone.

"Alex? Where are you?"

"I'm buying clothes for everyone. I should be there in half an hour tops."

"All right. Make it quick, ok?"

"Sure. Is something the matter?"

There's a pause, so I know there must be something.

"It's Lori. She's not doing too good. I want to take her to the hospital."

"Is she ok? She was fine last night!"

"She's not recovering like she should be, and there's nothing here I can help her with. I think she needs a doctor."

Shit.

"Has she got all her good papers?"

"Yeah, she's all right. And it looks like an animal bite so they won't call the cops, you have nothing to worry about."

"Good."

The last thing I need is trouble with the cops, especially since I'm sure I must have left some fingerprints at the Exxxotic. Of course, the only dead bodies that they could have found are either still moving and talking or great big piles of dust, but you don't get to where I am by taking chances. Still, Lori's my responsibility, in more respects than just the obvious one.

"I'm on my way. I'll give you cash to take the others to a hotel, and I'll take her to the hospital."

"You sure? You'll have to talk to doctors."

I sigh, annoyed. Luke does know me too well. But I'd rather spend a couple minutes talking to doctors than answer the kids' questions or face the fear and uncertainty in their eyes. Besides which, I can't drive the bus. I reach the cash register with the stuff I'm buying.

"Yeah, yeah, I'm sure. Is she ok for another fifteen minutes?"

"Make it quick."

I hang up and put the phone in my pocket. The cashier is looking at me weird, scanning the dozen or so identical garments while chewing her bubble gum. She's nothing but a kid, though she's probably the same age as Lori. She looks immature and spoiled, and there's no way she was the one that paid for the clothes she's wearing. I glare at her with all my resentment, and at least she stops looking so insolent. She doesn't even look at me weird or whine about the change in her cash when I pay for the clothes using only hundred dollar bills.

Jimmy's car is still in the driveway when I get to Erik's place, but I tell the cab to wait for me anyway. He was drinking whiskey when I left him there, after all. He knows I hate it when he's drunk in front of me, but he might have thought it didn't count, since I wasn't there. There's someone sitting on the steps smoking a cigarette, and I recognize Lori by her posture before I can even see the color of her hair. I light my smoke when I get close to her. I actually manage to use my power on my own this time.

She looks up when she sees me and she looks like hell. She's pale as death, and there are huge bags and dark circles under her eyes.

"Hey, Alex."

"Hey, Lori. You ok?"

She shrugs and takes another drag on her cigarette.

"I dunno. Luke's worried. I just feel so tired and weak. And I keep puking."

I try to stop myself, but I make a face anyway.

"Sorry. I'm just gonna go see Luke and I'll take you to the hospital."

She grins at me.

"You're gonna be my big strong hero?"

It takes me aback, and I feel my cheeks start heating. I throw my cigarette out and rush inside before the blush starts to show. I run into Kim and Lucy talking quietly in a corner of the entrance hall. They look scared when the door opens, but when they recognize me, they relax immediately. Lucy stays there hugging her blue stuffed bear, but Kim gets up and comes to hug me. I hug her back, awkwardly. She might be the second youngest but she's not usually this demonstrative. None of them are very fond of physical affection, of course, and it always surprises me, especially when I don't know what prompted it.

"Hey, girls. Everything ok?"

Kim gives me a smile. She's still wearing her white and pink pajamas. I guess I should be thankful that this all happened during summer.

"Where did you go?"

"I went to buy you guys some clothes so you wouldn't have to walk around in your pajamas."

I tap her shoulder a bit awkwardly; I'm not good with touching, either. I reach into the big plastic bag with the clothes in, and hand the girls each a pair of blue shorts and a white t-shirt, along with a pair of underwear and sports socks. Lucy makes a face at the clothes, but Kim laughs at them as she takes them.

"Alex! These are really ugly! I thought you had taste."

"I do have taste!"

She shakes her head at me, trying to look serious but failing.

"You don't. You're even worse than Luke. These are proof."

I straighten up. She can always make me smile.

"Ah, then I suppose I don't have the good taste to give Luke lots of money to take you guys shopping."

Her eyes light up. Lucy's do too. She hasn't spoken to anyone other than Kim since the days of the brothel, but she communicates with her expressions, whether she knows it or not. I leave them to it and head further in towards the kitchen. I only make it as far as the living room, though. Luke is there, putting a blanket on Jimmy, who's sprawled on the couch snoring. So much for not getting drunk around me. I dump the suit I had borrowed from him in the hallway. Luke looks up at me when he hears me come in, and then he walks towards me.

"Hey. Did you find Lori?"

"Yeah, I wanted to bring you these."

I toss him the bag of clothes, and he catches it.

"You still got the rest of the money from the safe?"

He nods, looking through the bag.

"Yeah, I do. I don't think the girls will like what you picked, though."

"That's why I want you to take them shopping. Buy them something nice, and then check into a hotel. Not the Grand hotel, but a nice one with a pool. Ok?"

He nods. He looks happy with my decision.

"Sounds good. How long will we be staying?"

I sigh. Hotels get expensive fast, especially with that amount of guests. I'm going to have to see if I can fix the house, and how fast.

"I don't know. Can I leave it to you to find out how damaged the house is, and to hire contractors?"

He nods again. Thank goodness I have Luke to help; he's a genius, the real kind. He was the one that forged the deeds to the brothel house after we took it over, to make it so I owned it. Nobody was going to claim it anyway, not like the homes of the guys we had killed, that went to their families. Still, Luke made sure the mortgage was paid and nobody was sticking their nose in. He made sure the kids had clothes, and food, and that everything ran well, while I made sure the mobs left us alone.

He glances at Jimmy when he's done going through the bag, and then looks back up at me with a doubtful expression.

"He's not going to drive you."

"I have a cab waiting. Reminds me, I should go. Meter's running."

"Good. Keep me posted."

I nod at him and turn around to walk out. The girls aren't in the hall anymore, probably went to get changed, but Lori's still outside, still smoking. She grins at me.

"Are we finally going? I think your driver's asleep."

I look up. She's right. The guy's reclining in his seat, eyes closed, mouth open. I can't believe I'm paying him for this.

"Yeah, we're going. You ok to walk?"

She shrugs, and stands really shakily, so I let her lean on me as we walk to the car. I bang on the hood to wake the driver up and he jerks awake in a very satisfying manner. I open the door for Lori and make sure she's sitting comfortably before I get in on the other side.

AUGUST 31ST, 2:17 PM

It's nice that I have to leave the doctors alone with Lori while they do their examination because it gives me time to wash my face and brush my hair. I still have to wait even when I'm done with all that, so I go to the cafeteria and find us the least objectionable sandwiches they have, some kind of chicken salad. When I get back up to where she is, the nurse tells me I can finally go in.

The room is kinda small, but it's nice and private. I picked a good hospital, since I can afford to pay for it anyway. She's wearing a clean hospital gown, and the bandages around her neck are newer and better made than the ones Luke had put on. She's hooked up to two IVs, one of clear fluid and one of blood. Her face is less pale than it was, but her eyes look red and puffy. Is she just tired, or has she been crying?

"Hey Lori. I brought you a sandwich."

She stares at the window, not even looking up at me. She stays quiet. I wonder what's wrong with her. I've seen her go through horrible things without even batting an eye. I find a chair and pull it up close to the bed. I offer her the sandwich, but she's still not acknowledging me, much less reaching to take it.

"It's chicken, so it's like, healthy and low-fat and stuff."

She doesn't move.

"Lori?"

I lower the arm that's holding the sandwich.

"What's wrong?"

She turns to me, but she can't sustain my stare. She looks down at her hands, folded in her lap.

"They did some tests... to figure out why I was feeling so sick. They said it couldn't just be the blood loss."

"Ok..."

I wait for her to go on, because I have no idea what she wants to say.

"They discovered... something."

"What?"

I'm worried suddenly. Is she sick? Does she have cancer or AIDS or something? I hope not. I think that, no matter how messed up I feel about her, I'd miss her if she were gone. She picks up the blanket and starts removing lint from it, methodically.

"I'm pregnant, Alex."

I feel around with my hand to find a chair to sit on, and then I remember that I already am sitting. So why do I feel like I'm falling?

"...what?"

She glares at me briefly and shakes her head, looking away. I think I see tears in her eyes again.

"You heard me."

I look down at the sandwich. It looks revolting to me, suddenly. Funny. I was so hungry a minute ago. I try to think. What am I supposed to say? Is it mine? How can I even know that? I mean, I know how babies are made, I'm not an idiot, but I'm fuzzy on the details, 'cause I never really made it past fifth grade, being on the streets and all. She sniffles and wipes her eyes, and glowers at me again.

"Well? Aren't you going to say something?"

I look up at her. I've never seen her distraught before, not about anything. When I first met her, she'd been beaten by a john so badly that Luke told me he wasn't sure she was going to walk again, but she just made jokes about it. Not now. If she really does have feelings to hurt, I don't wanna be the one to hurt them.

"I don't know what I'm supposed to say."

"You know it's yours, right?"

I stare at her. I can't help it. Is she telling me I'm going to be a father? I don't want to be a father. What if I turn out to be just like mine?

"You're sure?"

She throws her hands up in the air.

"Of course I'm sure! I haven't slept with anyone else in like, forever!"

I want to light a cigarette, and I see that I still have the sandwiches in my hands, so I put them down on the table next to her. I take out the silver cigarette case, but I decide not to take out a smoke. She's still looking at me, but I still don't know what to say to her.

"Well? Say something!"

I don't know what my face looks like right now, but she looks at it for a few seconds and she breaks down in tears, covering hers with her hands. I drag my chair closer to her. I have to say something now. I hope it'll be the right thing.

"Hey... there's no need to be afraid. I... I'm gonna take care of you. Both of you."

She looks at me, hiccupping a bit, trying to control her sobs.

"Really? You want to... and be with me?"

I don't know what I want, but I'm not going to tell her that. She needs me. And I'm responsible, I guess.

"Sure. Don't worry."

She sniffles and nods again. She steals furtive looks at me. I know what she wants, so I stand. My body feels like lead, but I can make it move anyway. I walk to the side of the bed, and she leans her head against my chest. I wrap my arms around her loosely while she clings to my shirt with her fingers.

AUGUST 31ST, 6:47 PM

The motel Luke picked is definitely not the Grand Hotel, but I guess I've seen worse. It looks clean, at least, and there's nothing dead in the pool; it's even open, the kids are in it. The taxi drops us off at the gate. Lori hasn't said anything for the whole ride, just clung to me like she was afraid I'd disappear. She's still doing it now, as we head towards the pool where the youngest kids are playing. Like that, from here, they look almost like normal kids, playing in the water, splashing each other and throwing an inflatable ball around. Luke is watching over them. He stands and comes towards me when he sees me heading his way. He meets me at the gate, out of earshot from the kids. They haven't noticed me yet, so I try to stay out of their sight.

Luke looks Lori over quickly but carefully when we meet, only briefly nodding at me.

"Hey Lori. How are you feeling?"

She shrugs, and gets closer to me.

"Ok, I guess."

I try to smile at her, and pull a couple hundred bucks out of my jacket pocket.

"Why don't you go get a room? You could use the rest."

She takes the money, but hesitantly, like she doesn't really want it.

"Will you come join me later?"

"Yeah, sure. You go ahead and get some sleep, ok?"

She nods a bit and heads towards the front desk. I watch her go, then turn to glance at the kids. Some of them have noticed me; Kim is waving. I wave back.

"Can we go somewhere to talk?"

Luke looks back at the kids and nods, leading me away from the pool, to a little spot under the second story walkway where there are vending machines and a bench. I sit on the bench, but he goes to the machine to get a candy bar and a soda.

"I went by the house. It's not too bad, there was a lot of smoke damage but the worst is the water damage from when they put out the fire. I think we should get by pretty easily with the insurance."

I frown at him, perplexed.

"We have insurance?"

"Yeah, we do."

He gives me a proud grin. I shake my head, but I have to admit I'm relieved to hear it, and more than a little impressed. There's a reason why I trust him to run things in that place.

"Good, good. Listen, I want you to bring the kids inside before sunset."

"Yeah, right, no problem. You weren't joking with that vampire crap, were you?"

I shake my head. He should know I don't joke. There's squealing in the pool and I look up sharply, half ready to go and defend them, but I hear laughter in the same high-pitched voice, and I realize they're only playing, so I relax.

"Are they ok?"

Luke glances at me and then goes back to watching the pool, opening his can of cherry soda.

"You mean about last night? Well, some are a little shaken, but they're ok. Kim tells me Lucy worries about you."

"Tell them I'm fine."

He looks at me again and chuckles.

"Yeah, tell it to your face."

I sigh. The bruise is almost healed, so it's looking its worst right now, all black and yellow, so I see what he means. They keep seeing me injured these days, and before this business is over, I'm sure I'll get banged around a bit more. Which is another reason to do what I've decided to do.

"Luke... when the house is fixed, I won't be moving back in with you guys."

He frowns at me, but he doesn't look that shocked.

"Oh?"

"Yeah. These guys... they were after me. I got no right to be putting you guys in so much danger. The business I run, the powers I have... it's not safe to be around me. And besides... I don't like that they worry about me. They're too young to worry."

He laughs again.

"Some of them are older than you, Alex."

"Shut up. I got responsibilities."

I glare at him, but as usual, it doesn't faze him. He just shakes his head at me.

"And we don't? Look, Alex. You have to let off a bit of the pressure you put on yourself. You can't protect them all the time. Besides, they've already seen much worse than what they've got coming to them for the rest of their lives, I assure you."

I don't answer. I know what he's saying. Some of them, like Jimmy, like Lucy and Lori, they're damaged goods. I guess we all are, really. It doesn't change the fact that I want the rest of their lives to be different. Not just a little, like getting back on top of the situation like Jimmy did, but a lot, like going to college and getting married and all those things. And I understand that it means some of us have to make sacrifices, and will never have those things, like Jimmy, like Luke. Like me.

Luke watches me for a little while more, drinking his soda, and he sighs when he finally understands I'm not gonna answer.

"I get what you're doing, though, and I respect it. We'll always keep you a room in the house, that's for sure. And don't stop visiting, either. These kids love you, they look up to you, even more than you imagine. The guys all want to be like you, and the girls all want to marry you."

I sigh. That's another thing; I wouldn't wish my life on anyone, and no one should wish to share it. Not even someone as messed up as Lori. Lori. Shit. What am I gonna do?

"Right. Well tell them they should find someone who doesn't have to burn things and beat people up in the course of their jobs. And someone who's at least finished grade school."

"You're too hard on yourself. Don't you realize what you did for us? What, do you think that you'd have done it better with a degree and a nice job?"

"Maybe. I dunno. Whatever."

I lean my head in my hands. He doesn't understand, but that's to be expected. He didn't go to school either, though he was smart enough to learn by himself from books and computers and stuff. I guess he doesn't realize how ignorant those of us who are stupid like me can be.

He drinks the rest of his soda, watching the kids in silence, while I sink in a darker and darker mood, until I can't stand myself anymore.

"Well, I guess I better go check on Lori. Will you keep an eye on her when I'm not there? She's going through a lot."

He frowns at me before tossing his empty can in the trash.

"Is she ok? She looked better than she did this morning, but..."

"Yeah... I think she'll be ok."

He unwraps his candy bar, taking a quick look towards the kids to make sure they're all right. They are, of course, the pool's not that deep and most of them are in their mid-teens, so they can take care of themselves. Besides, there's a lifeguard there. He starts eating the chocolate, watching me.

"You got something on your mind. What is it?"

I can't get anything by him, but I guess that's ok. I'm treading on unknown territory here, and I think I could at least use his advice.

"She's pregnant."

His eyes widen and his eyebrows shoot up, his jaw becoming slack; I can see the half-chewed chocolate and peanuts through his teeth. He swallows without chewing any further before talking.

"Is it..."

"Mine? Yeah."

"Wow."

We sit there quietly while he eats the rest of his candy bar, keeping an eye on the pool. I know it's big, so I give him time to process it.

"So, what are you gonna do?"

I make a face at him. I didn't expect something so inane and ignorant from this guy. What does that mean, what am I gonna do?

"What are you talking about?"

"Well... does she want to keep it?"

"I guess. She says she wants to be with me."

"And you?"

"What, and me?"

"Well, do you love her?"

"Aren't you listening? She's having my kid! Who the fuck cares whether or not I love her?"

He scratches the back of his head, puffing his cheeks and releasing the air through tight lips slowly.

"Well... it's kinda important."

I let out an annoyed sigh again. Why can't he just understand? I'm not asking about love, I'm asking about becoming a father.

"This isn't about love, it's about responsibility. And my ability to raise a kid, good and proper."

Or lack thereof, I should say. I don't, though. I've shown enough weakness to Luke to last me two lifetimes. He shakes his head, smiling. Great. He thinks I've said something stupid again.

"It is so about love. If you love her, and the kid, you'll do a good job. It's bastards without love who raise kids like us."

I get the cigarette case from the pocket of my jacket and light one. I don't even need to think about it, really, I'm so annoyed.

"I guess I don't hate her."

He chuckles.

"That's at least a start."

"Anyway, I guess I better go check on her before I go."

His smile disappears, and he frowns at me. He looks a little worried.

"Where are you gonna go?"

I shrug. I hadn't really thought that far, really, but I gotta keep on the move. I'll go nuts if I don't do anything.

"I don't know yet. I guess I'm gonna go find Jimmy and Erik and discuss where we're gonna go from here."

"Alex... be careful. These guys are seriously messed up. They're bad news, even for you."

"They attacked our home, Luke."

He sighs, but he doesn't say anything else. I think he understands. I finish my cigarette as I head to the stairs, but I realize Lori hasn't told me which room she'd be in, so I figure I might as well let her sleep. She'll probably call me.

AUGUST 31ST, 8:42 PM

Jimmy's car is still in the driveway when I get to Erik's place. That could be good, or bad, I suppose, though I think Erik would have the good sense to get rid of the car if he'd killed him. I tip the cabbie and go to the house, walking in without knocking. If my friend's there, being polite doesn't matter; if not, I want the element of surprise. I hear Jimmy laugh when I come in, though. It's not something I've heard much since I met him, especially something this sincere. Then, I hear Erik's voice.

"Someone's just come in. Hey, Alex, is that you? We're in the kitchen."

I close the door behind me and walk to the kitchen. There's a smell that reminds me of barbecue, and I see that Jimmy is eating an enormous rack of baby back ribs while Erik is chatting casually. They're both having beer.

"Hey Alex! Your vampire friend is pretty cool."

I frown at him suspiciously; he's never been this expressive about someone before, except for when he hates them.

"Did he make you into one of them?"

They look at each other and both burst out laughing. I guess he seems all right, so I relax. He licks his fingers, then wipes his hands on his jeans and pushes the rest of his ribs towards me. There's a lot left, they're still warm, and I never ended up eating those stupid chicken sandwiches, so I dig in.

"Got your affairs in order, then?"

Erik is grinning that annoying grin at me.

"Well, the kids are outta here, aren't they?"

He shrugs.

"I guess they are. Wanna beer?"

"No. I don't drink."

"Right, you like the soda. I think you drank all I had. My tap works, though. I can get you some water if you like."

"That's ok."

"So, have you just come here to pick up your friend, or are you hiding out here?"

I glare at him. Why does he have to read me so well? He hardly knows me at all, and I sure can't read him half as well.

"I'm not hiding! I've come to discuss what we do next."

"I guess I can understand that you wouldn't want to stay away from them now."

"Little hard, when they won't stay away from me."

"So what do you intend to do, then?"

"Take them out. All of them. I won't have that scum in my town. And you'll help me do it."

He looks surprised but amused at the same time.

"Oh, I will, will I?"

"Yeah, you will. You got no love for these guys. And if I'm right, if they really are trying to take control of this town, they'll need to take you out sooner or later, won't they?"

"I suppose they will."

"Then it's settled. Strength in numbers, all that crap. Right, Jimmy?"

Jimmy nods at Erik, taking a sip of his beer.

"It's a good point."

"All right, I'll help you. So what do you need?"

"I need you to tell me about these guys. The leaders. Who are they? Where'd they come from? What do you think their next move will be?"

He looks at both Jimmy and me, and then just shrugs and goes to the fridge to get out two more beers. He tosses one to Jimmy and opens the second one.

"The leader is really young, but just old enough to have gained real confidence in himself and his little schemes, about fifty, give or take. So he's still a beginner, far from full strength yet."

Fifty years? I lose track of the conversation for a moment. That's pretty damn old. But he says it's brand new. How old is this guy? I come back to it in the middle of a phrase.

"...and so he's one of the first promoters of the lifestyle, even though others figured it out on their own later."

"The lifestyle?"

I didn't catch the beginning of the phrase, so I have no idea what he's talking about. He shakes his head, but he doesn't actually look annoyed.

"Yeah. You know, living comfortably, controlling businesses, making money."

"You guys didn't make money before?"

"Well, we stole it. And we didn't spend it much. It's a little complicated, and not really relevant. You wanna let me finish?"

"Yeah, yeah."

"Anyway, he wanted better for himself. So he broke his master's control, and started testing his theory, moving from city to city across Europe until he gathered enough help and practice to make it work."

"Did he make it work?"

"Well, at first, no. But eventually he settled somewhere in Italy, and he built up an impressive organization, until eventually he took over the whole city of Napoli. I mean Naples."

"So why is he here?"

"To be honest, I'm not sure. But the clan he booted out of Naples was old and really well established. They were taken by surprise, of course, but I know they had ties elsewhere. Who knows, maybe they overthrew this little gang again to take back what was theirs."

I try to think while he takes a break to sip at his beer. It seems to fit. Lupino's from Italy, and from what he says happened to his family, and how long ago...

"Hey, do you know if there's a vampire in their gang called Nicola?"

He seems to think hard for a second.

"Yeah, I think he's in charge. Ruthless guy, pretty cruel?"

I glance at Jimmy. Jimmy doesn't like Lupino; he always says he's gotta be working an angle with me, even if I don't think so. It doesn't matter, I decide. I'll say it anyway, and to hell with Jimmy and his opinions of Lupino.

"That Nicola guy... I think he's my boss's son."

"Really? Hmm."

Erik rubs his chin, frowning, as if lost in thought. Jimmy's staring at me, though.

"That guy's son is a vampire?"

"Well, I don't really think you can blame him, do you?"

"Whatever."

Jimmy shakes his head in apparent discouragement and Erik has a decisive nod.

"Well, it would explain why they've chosen to come here."

"Are you saying you think he came here because of his father?"

"It's more than likely."

"Do you think... like... does he remember who he is?"

He makes a face and drinks his beer.

"What do you mean?"

"I mean, why do you think he's come to find his father? Is it because he remembers him? Could he miss him?"

"He probably does remember him. But if he did come for him, it's not for anything good, that's for sure."

"Oh."

That's just too bad. It would have been great to be able to bring Lupino's son back to him.

"Why would he come now, though? I mean, it's been a really, really long time, like thirty years, or something."

Erik seems to think that what I just said is funny, but he doesn't comment other than answer my question.

"Like I said, when you're first turned, you have a period of servitude to the one who changed you. It could just be that he finally broke free, and this is the first thing he decided to do."

"So what's the best plan to get these guys?"

He looks at me, and downs the last of his beer in a single gulp.

"All right. I think they're holing up at Fellini's right now."

Jimmy raises an eyebrow.

"The nightclub? That's a change from strip joints. You sure they're not still at the Exxxotic?"

He shakes his head.

"You attacked them there. They're confident, but not stupid. Well, not that stupid anyway. They're going to have moved, and I keep pretty good track of them."

"All right. So what, do we just show up there and torch the place?"

Jimmy nods his approval, but Erik shakes his head.

"Not just like that. You need a more solid plan. If they're holed up there, it means the place has sewer access. Now the best way is to go through there during the day, cut off their access. Then you torch the place, and you make sure none of them escape."

It's so simple. I don't know why I never thought of it before. I shake my head.

"I guess it does help to have an insider in this. You'll come with us tomorrow?"

"Sure. Meet me here. But you guys are gonna have to let me get some rest first, though. Couldn't exactly go to sleep with all you and yours all over the place."

"Fine, fine. C'mon, Jimmy. You're driving me back."

He nods, and shakes Erik's hand. That's a real mark of affection coming from Jimmy.

"Thanks for the whiskey, man. It was grand."

"I got more where that came from, don't you worry."

Erik claps him on the upper arm, and Jimmy leads the way outside. This time, he walks us all the way to the door.

"So where are you staying now?"

"A motel."

"Good. Don't let too many people know the exact location for now, and you shouldn't let them go back to your old place until this is all resolved."

"I know how to take care of my people."

He chuckles and taps my shoulder.

"You sure are wound tight, kid."

"Maybe it's 'cause of assholes like you calling me 'kid' all the time."

"Try to relax! You might actually enjoy your life."

I shrug him off and follow Jimmy outside. As soon as we're away from the door, he gestures for me to give him a smoke. I do and take one for myself, and we climb into his car.

"You didn't tell me that guy was cool."

"Since when do you think anybody's cool?"

"I always thought you were cool. You jealous?"

He grins insolently at me as he backs out of the driveway.

"Of course not. Just... I've never seen you get along with anyone so fast, that's all."

"You know, he's right. You are wound pretty tight."

"Keep your comments to yourself."

He laughs and drives. I don't talk to him anymore except to give him the name of the motel, and he gets the hint, staying quiet too, just putting on his favorite blues radio station at a low volume to let me think.

AUGUST 31ST, 10:31 PM

I use the key Luke gave me to open the door to Lori's room. He said she was fine, and that he checked on her earlier and that she was watching TV. I didn't stay to ask any more questions, because he had half the kids in his room eating pizza and watching a movie.

She's lying on the bed, sleeping. She didn't take off any of her clothes, or even her shoes. I expected there to be two beds, too, but there's just one, a small table and an open kitchen. At least, there's a couch. I put down my stuff on the table and go to the bathroom to have a shower.

It's right there, all over the bathroom counter, the needle, the rubber tube, the plastic Ziploc bag full of powder. She didn't even bother to hide it. And it's not like she was getting rid of it, either. I can see the spoon she used to heat it.

All thoughts of showers gone, I stomp back in the room to shake her awake. She blinks at me, confused; I can see in her eyes that she's not all there.

"What? What do you want?"

I give her a hard shake, and she whimpers.

"What have you done, you stupid cow! You got high!"

"So what? Leave me alone, you don't own me!"

She tries to shake me off, but she's high, and I'm much stronger than she is.

"You're pregnant! Are you too stupid to realize what you've done to your baby?"

She glares at me, but stops struggling.

"So what? I can do what I want, you don't decide!"

Her eyes widen, looking to my right, and she gasps and yelps. That's when I realize my right hand is up, ready to come down and hit her. I let go of her and stagger back. The anger's not far, but right now, I suddenly feel sick. I was going to hit a helpless girl. A helpless girl who's the mother of my child.

I run to the bathroom, and throw myself in front of the toilet to throw up. I shouldn't have wondered; I'm exactly the monster that he was. And worse, I don't even need to be drunk.

I stagger to the sink once I'm done, and I see the bag again. I pick it up and empty it in the toilet. It makes me feel a bit better, but not much.

She's still awake when I walk out, her eyes wide and fearful. I can't look at her, so I just get out of the room. I don't know where I'm gonna go. I go to the stairs and sit, lighting a cigarette. My eyes sting. I try to prevent the tears from forming, but this time it takes a lot more effort, and my breathing becomes heavy with it, but, as always, I manage to keep the tears away, even though it makes my ribs hurt. I haven't cried since I was twelve years old, and I intend to keep it that way. By the time I'm finished smoking my first cigarette, I feel better. Halfway through my second, the door to Luke's room opens, and four of the girls come out. I try to make myself discreet, but there's no need. I'm sitting, and in the shadows, so they don't have time to notice me by the time they reach their room, two doors down from Luke's. He leans out the door to make sure they get to their destination like the responsible adult that he is, and then he turns towards me like he knew I was there. By the way he squints, though, I can tell he's not sure if it's me.

"Alex? Is that you?"

I stand, and nod. I'm divided between running away and coming closer. I don't really wanna share my feelings, but I think my head will explode if I'm left alone with my thoughts.

"Yeah, it's me."

"Everything ok? Why aren't you in your room?"

He comes out of his, closing the door behind him, and comes closer to me.

"Did Lori come on to you again?"

I turn away from him, reaching for another cigarette. I try not to let the silver case remind me of her, but it's hard, and I don't trust my voice to speak, so I just shake my head.

"What happened?"

"She... she got high."

"Oh. Shit, Alex, I'm sorry. I don't know where she got the stuff, she looked fine all evening."

"It's not your fault. You can't watch all of them at once, and you gotta keep a closer eye on the young ones."

My voice is surprisingly steady, but I keep taking deep breaths anyway to keep it under control. He keeps giving me that worried look, though, and I feel really annoyed.

"You're really worried about the baby, aren't you."

"Of course I am! It's a kid! It'll be a person, like you, and like me! It deserves to be treated right!"

I can see the look in Lori's eyes again. I can't believe I almost hit her. I feel a wave of nausea and pain wash over me, and I sit back down to try and calm myself.

Luke sits next to me, one step lower, so that he has to crane his neck to look at me, but I sort of have no choice but to be looking at him.

"Look, Alex... I can't tell you that Lori's going to be the best mother in the world. She has her problems, and they run pretty deep. But you... I can't imagine a better father. You have nothing to worry about, I assure you."

I shake my head.

"You don't know. How could you know?"

"Come on. You didn't have to take care of any of us. You could have just left that place. And even if you did care enough to free us, you didn't have to stick around and make sure we were all right, or to provide us with a roof over our head and food on our table. Granted, you could be a little more expressive in your affections, but other than that, you're already doing a great job with difficult kids who aren't even yours."

I stare at my feet so I don't have to look in his face. How can I tell him what I've done? But I have to. Anyway, I'd rather say it than have her tell him.

"Luke..."

Mercifully, my phone rings at that very moment. I almost drop it in the stairs in my rush to pick up.

"Yeah?"

"Alex! Are you ok?"

It's Jimmy. He sounds breathless and agitated, if not to say frantic.

"What? Of course I'm ok. What are you talking about? What's going on?"

"That fucker! He came to my place and he attacked me! He's one of them!"

"What? What fucker?"

Is he talking about Erik? Did he double-cross us, somehow?

"Jack! He was waiting for me in front of my door! He got turned into one of those fucking things!"

I feel the blood drain from my face, and a cold chill runs down my spine. Jack?

"You mean, Mister Lupino's Jack?"

"Who else, fuck head? He's gonna come after you next!"

"Listen, are you ok, are you safe?"

"Yeah, I'm fine. I cut the bastard's throat so bad I nearly took off his head. I would have, too, if I'd had a decent knife. He's gone, now."

"Ok. Get yourself to a safe place. I'll call you later."

"What are you gonna do?"

"Call Lupino."

I hang up on him, and dial Lupino's number. My fingers shake, and Luke looks up at me, worried.

"What's going on?"

I put the phone against my ear after pressing send before answering him.

"One of Lupino's men has been turned. Get inside and make sure to keep an eye on the kids. You don't open the door for anyone, not even someone you know, especially if they have to ask if they can come in, you hear? He came after Jimmy."

Luke nods, and jogs up the stairs and across the walkway, starting to knock on all the kids' doors. I get Lupino's voicemail, so I call a taxi immediately, promising a hundred dollar tip if the cab's there in less than five minutes. If Lupino's in danger, I'm not taking a single chance.

AUGUST 31ST, 11:17 PM

I try reaching Lupino on his home phone, and again on his cell phone, all the way through the cab ride. Halfway there I do get the idea to call for reinforcements, though, and I could shout for joy if I wasn't such a nervous wreck as Erik answers his phone. I tell him to get his ass to Lupino's house, and he doesn't question, so I get a couple more opportunities to try and reach Lupino. There's still no answer. If he's dead, or hurt in any way, it doesn't matter how strong or supernatural they are. They're gonna pay.

The lights are on upstairs, but the first floor is dark. I give the cabbie too much money 'cause I can't be bothered with change, and run out of the car. When I get to the door, I see that it's ajar. There's not a sound inside.

"Mister Lupino?"

There's a thump upstairs, but no answer. I better not be too late. I fly up the stairs, probably taking them two at a time; I don't even know, and I can't feel the pain in my ribs anymore. I hate myself too much. How did I not see this coming? Of course they were after him. The Lupino group controls most of the city. If they want to dominate the city's underworld, they would have to make a move on him.

The hallway is dark, but I can see the light spilling from under the door of his office. It's open, but just by a bit. I stop in the hall and look around, but there doesn't seem to be anyone anywhere else. I try to make the fire, but worry was never a big motivator for me using my power, so I chase it away from my mind. I'm here now, whatever's happened has already happened, and there's nothing I can do about it except get revenge. The hatred is clear in my mind when I push the door open with my left hand, and the fire is just at my fingertips. That's when I see him, and I lose my concentration completely.

He's sitting on the floor in front of his desk. There's blood running down the side of his face; I can't tell if he's still conscious or not. He seems smaller, shorter somehow; I don't wanna say frail, but that's just because he's always been so larger than life that the word hurts my mind. He moves a bit, raising his head to look at me. I'm so glad he's alive I take a step forward, but then old habits kick in and I remember to check the room. Damn my stupid sentimentality.

They seem to come out of nowhere, and suddenly they're between me and Lupino. I start backing away and getting ready, but they're just standing there, grinning at me. I recognize Jack easily, though the jagged, healing cut on his throat and the blood-soaked shirt throw me for a second. He doesn't seem too bothered by it, though he does look pretty pissed off. He's standing over Lupino, and the old man looks scared. The expression on his face is so naked I can barely look at it, and I turn my attention to the other monster, the one I've met and fought and lost to before, the one that used to be Lupino's son. I hate him for that almost as much as for everything else he's done.

I almost don't notice the third one, not that he matters anyway; I don't think I've seen him before. He's pinned to the wall, next to the window, held in place by what looks to be two arrows. I see the crossbow on the floor not too far from Lupino, and it brings me a little happiness. The old man may be down, but he went down fighting. As he should.

The monster who was Lupino's son looks relaxed, and completely oblivious to the man who used to be his father behind him. His attention is on me, and he seems to be in the mood for talking. That's weird. I wait for him to start; if he's got something to say, then let him say it. I refuse to be intimidated by that fucker just 'cause he's got super speed and super strength and the power to suck me dry in a few minutes.

"Ah! Magic fire man. I must say, you are every bit as unimpressive now as you were when we first fought."

His accent is much thicker than Mister Lupino's; this guy sounds like he's fresh off the boat. I don't say anything. I won't let myself be baited like this, but at least I can use the anger to spark up my fire again. I have to make my move carefully though; Jack has Mister Lupino by the hair and chin, and now that he's one of them, he could just snap the old man's neck before I have any real chance at all. So I bide my time.

The monster in front of me folds his arms, and leans on one leg. If I'd been even a little gullible, or I didn't know what he was, he might have seemed friendly. He seems to wait for me to say something or get pissed off at him, and when I do nothing, he at least has the decency to look a little miffed.

He turns to look at Jack. Jack looks the same as he did in life; not as pale as what used to be Lupino's son, but I guess maybe that comes with time. He has the same dispassionate expression he always has, even when getting ready to kill the man who made him who he is. The man who, by all accounts, did as much for him as he ever did for me.

The moment seems to last forever. I can barely hold on to the fire; and even if I did, what could I do? I will not risk Lupino's life. Not for anything. The old man has his eyes closed. He looks ready to die; I've seen that look on many different faces, I'm sure I've had it on my own face more than once. But it's not going to happen. The monster turns to look at me again. I don't like his smile. Not that I like anything else about him.

"You seem to be hesitating. Is the old man so important to you?"

I refuse to answer, to do anything, and though I try to fight it as much as I can, I feel the expression on my face betray me. His smile widens, and he looks at his fingernails, trying to be casual. He doesn't fool me, though.

"We would be willing to let him live what little time he has left, on one condition."

Jack twists Lupino's head as far as it'll go without his neck breaking, and the old man lets out a whimper, despite himself, through clenched lips. I listen. I barely dare to breathe. I don't want to give him any more than he already has, the bastard. He watches me for a reaction, gets none, this time, and goes on.

"If you surrender to us willingly, we will let him go."

I must look surprised, because he looks amused. It's me they want? Over Lupino? I'm not sure that makes sense, with what Erik said, unless... Where is that guy, anyway? Does he even have a car? Damn him to hell. I can't wait for him anymore.

I try to think of something to do. Can I burn Jack like I did the others, in the bar? Would he still have time to snap Mister Lupino's neck? If I do, and the other one attacks me, am I sure to win? I have to be sure, if I'm going to be any help at all.

I take too much time; the guy is starting to look annoyed.

"I do not have all night. Decide now, or you both die."

I hear a grinding sound, and realize it's me gritting my teeth. I have to save the old man, but what about the others? What about Lori? I clench my fists. Luke will know what to do; I gave him ample instructions. Hopefully, he told everyone.

"Fine," I hear myself say, through clenched teeth. "Do your worst."

He grins. He's won, and he knows it, the bastard. All I can do is watch him come closer, his lips parted in an obnoxiously satisfied grin. I can see the sharpness of his teeth under it. They're not tiny little pointed fangs like in the movies; it's all his teeth that seem longer, and sharper, somehow. I guess it explains how mangled my neck and arm got.

He grabs my shoulder and brings me closer. I resist his pull, but that only seems to make his smile bigger. It makes me sick when he pulls the bandage from my neck. His fingers are cold against my skin but it's the memories that churn my stomach. His hands were cold too. But this time, I can't make the fire, though it builds up in me so strong I feel like I'm the one who's burning inside out. I hear Lupino make a sound, but I can't open my eyes to look.

I brace myself for the bite, but instead, the breath goes out of me from some kind of impact, and I'm thrown to the floor. It's at least a few seconds before I have my wind and my mind back, during which time I hear the sounds of a very hasty battle, and I look around. Jack isn't next to the desk anymore, and for a moment I fear the worst, but I see Lupino's not there, either. There's a sort of clacking sound, and I spot him, a few feet away, shooting a crossbow at the window. The bolt plants itself in the frame, and I can't see what he was shooting at; it's gone already. I stand up, fire at the ready, ready to kill the one that's still standing, but I can't find him, either. All that's left is the guy on the wall, still impaled there by crossbow bolts. I look around the room again, this time more carefully. I hadn't seen them when I walked in; they could still be hiding.

I really can't see anyone from where I am, so I walk around, checking every corner, every piece of furniture. I stop at the window to look outside and shut it. I pick out the bolt sticking out of its frame. The shaft is wooden, with a mean-looking four-pointed metal head. The weapon of someone who means business, especially if dealing with this specific kind of unwelcome guest. I find Lupino. He's standing now, staring at the door. He looks pale, and shaken. His eyes are wide, and feverish, but I can see the man I know somewhere in there. I can't stand his haunted look, though; I gotta say something.

"So... crossbow, huh?"

Great. Now he's going to think I'm an idiot. At least, he doesn't seem to react. He looks down at his weapon like he didn't notice it before, and nods absently.

"It is good to be prepared for these... situations."

I look at the bolt again. I don't know much about that kind of gear, but I know enough to know that metal or fiberglass is generally popular, not wood. I guess the old man really must have known a thing or two.

Before I get a chance to ask, Erik walks through the door. Lupino has his crossbow up. I didn't even notice he'd reloaded it. Erik throws his hands up.

"Friendly target! I'm the one that just saved you, don't you remember?"

"It's all right, Mister Lupino, I know him. I'm the one who called him."

Lupino looks at me, frowning.

"Humans do not move like that, Alex."

"They don't make fire, either. Don't worry, I know him. He's on our side."

Mister Lupino hesitates a bit, but he lowers his crossbow. He looks alert and watchful, but I can see how tired he is. He doesn't look hurt, though, and his neck is intact. Erik lets his hands drop to his sides, smiling, with no visible relief, like he knew all along that Lupino would do that. I take a step forward, putting myself sort of between him and Lupino. I still have a few questions.

"How did you get in?"

Erik raises one of his eyebrows, like I said something funny.

"You invited me."

"I thought you could only be invited by people who live in the house."

"Well, yes."

"Well, I don't live here."

He shrugs dismissively.

"If I could come in on your invitation, you do."

I look at Mister Lupino. He looks a bit more relaxed, which only means his tired air is showing more. His attention turns from Erik to the vampire that's still pinned to the wall with two crossbow bolts. The thing is writhing, trying to pull out the bolts, but as it sees us focusing on it, it stops, and hisses at us. I notice it's looking at Lupino and me, not Erik, though. I wonder if that's significant. Doesn't really matter right now, though. I'm busy working up a good mad, the kind that has me just pissed off enough to make the fire but not so much that I lose control over its output. It doesn't even take a second, and by the time I'm within arm's reach of the vampire, I can feel the heat. I put on my most impressive face.

"Tell me what you want from us and where the others are hiding."

It hisses at me again, and then starts to laugh, saying something in a language I can't understand. It sounds a bit like Italian, but weird, and different. Lupino doesn't seem to understand, either, not exactly, though if I'm reading his face right, he's almost getting it, or remembering how to understand, like something he's learned a long time ago. Either way, I don't like people who insult me in languages I don't understand.

I'm about to say something back just to shut it up, but Erik beats me to it, answering it in the same language. The vampire hisses again and squirms, trying to get free of the crossbow bolts. I don't know if what Erik said was particularly offensive, but there sure seems to be bad blood between them. I'm sick of them not paying attention to me, though. Who's running this show, anyway? This time, I act before I speak, to make sure the vampire on the wall understands who's in charge here. I concentrate on his arms, which he's stretching out in front of him to try to grab Erik, or just be generally scary, and start heating the skin. Not enough so that they'll catch fire, I don't know how fast he'll turn to dust if I do that, but just enough so that the skin bubbles, and starts to crack. That gets his attention all right, he starts screaming, and thrashing around with no purpose.

I release the heat and take a step forward, careful to remain out of his reach; these bastards can be quick. Its eyes are fixed on me, and I can see the whites all around the irises, though it still looks more enraged than scared.

"Got your attention now? Good. You were about to tell me what your group wants from us, and where the others are hiding."

It hisses and writhes again, but I can tell this time it's scared more than just pissed off. Still, it doesn't answer me, so I get even more pissed, which can do nothing but help. Erik and Lupino are just watching me, so I go on.

"Listen carefully, freak. You're going to die here, you got no choice about that. But I can kill you with a snap of my fingers... or I can make it last all night, burn you inch by inch, if I want. Just depends on how pissed off you make me."

As I say the last part, I slowly bring the heat back in the same place as before. The thing moans and grits its teeth, but it can't hide how much this hurts. I don't stop, though. I always make it a point that my threats are never idle or empty. I have to admit, the thing has a seriously high pain threshold; three of its fingers have turned to ash by the time it screams for mercy. It doesn't have an accent, like I expected; then again, neither does Erik.

"Please! I'll talk, I swear!"

"I'm still not hearing anything I wanna hear."

"The others are hiding in the basement under Fellini's. Please, stop!"

Just like Erik said. I don't stop. I finally got him talking; I'm not about to stop. There's more I want to know.

"What do you want with us?"

"Just... to take the city!!"

That doesn't seem to make sense, after the way they've been acting. Erik jumps in before I get time to ask more questions, though.

"This is MY city, and you all know it. What do you really want here?"

I think his eyes turn to me, but after a few seconds, I realize it's Lupino he's looking at. It can't be him they were after; why offer to spare him if they got to turn me? Then again, I remember who it was that made the offer, and the facts start lining up, slowly, like those pictures that were made only of dots and numbers, but if you connected them in the right order, you'd get the drawing of something. Erik had said if this guy remembers his father, then he'd want nothing good.

"It's personal, isn't it? But nothing to do with Erik? This is about Mister Lupino's son, isn't it?"

Erik turns to look at me. His eyebrows are a bit raised, but it's hard to tell if he's impressed or just surprised. I try to steal a glance at Lupino, while looking like my attention is still on that thing on the wall. His eyes are down, and I can't read his expression. The vampire hisses at me, and squirms again. I'm thinking it'll just try to defy me again, but it starts talking.

"It's about revenge. It was Nicola who had us come here. The rest of us knew it was a bad idea, but he's in charge. Let me go!"

"Revenge for what?"

"I don't know, I swear! Just let me go!"

I can't tell if he's lying to me or not, so I give a quick look at Erik. He nods once, discreetly. It looks dismissive, like we're done, so I figure the thing really has told me all it knows. I face it again.

"The deal was, you talk, and I kill you quick. You held up your end."

It hisses at me again, but I can tell it has no more real fight left in it. I feel tired, suddenly, and not angry enough to make the fire, so I turn to Lupino, holding out my hand.

I almost don't look at him, and it's as well; I'm shocked by the way he looks. He's pale, and drained, like all the life's gone out of him. His eyes are bloodshot and glistening, and there are huge bags under them. He looks at my outstretched hand dazedly, and holds out the crossbow. I take it. I've never worked a medieval thing like that before, but it's got a trigger, and I'm point-blank, so it's not too hard to figure out. The thing bursts into dust and embers as the bolt goes through its heart, just like in the movies, and there's no trace that he ever was here except for the pile of gray powder on the floor. Lupino watches, but he's still got the same look on his face, and I can't tell what he's thinking, or if he's even seeing what's happening at all. He looks far away. I want to help, say something, but I suck at this stuff, and I don't want him to look weak in front of Erik. Fortunately, Erik spares me the trouble in a remarkably delicate method, for a cold-hearted bloodsucker.

"I think I left something in my car. I'll wait for you outside."

He walks out, leaving me with a few seconds to think about what I'm gonna say. As soon as he's out of sight, though, Lupino walks to his desk, slumping down in his chair. I stay where I am, watching him, wondering if he's going to say anything, but he sighs and puts his face in his hands, his whole body sagging. I don't know what to do or say, so I stay here. I think I see his shoulders shaking, and I look away. It's none of my business, anyway.

I finally walk to the desk to put the crossbow down on it; there's really no other flat surface in the room unless you count the top of the bookshelves, but you never know if we might need it again, and Mister Lupino's not that tall. I pull out one of the chairs facing him, trying to make as little noise as I can; happily for me, I'm more discreet than Jimmy. I wait for what seems like forever, but he doesn't look up at me, trapped in his own private grief for a moment. I try to imagine what he's feeling, but I don't even have a basis for comparison. Finally, I can't stand it anymore, I have to say something, anything, so I go for one of the most benign platitudes people say on that kind of occasion.

"Can I get you anything, Mister Lupino?"

I hate myself as soon as I've said it. What could I possibly get him that would ease his pain, or make any difference at all? He doesn't seem to mind, though, and it does bring him back, like it was all he was waiting for. He uses the hands that were already covering his face to wipe his eyes, and I look away to pretend I didn't notice, trying to find something interesting to look at. I don't find anything, but at least it keeps my mind busy until he's ready to answer me. I wanna ask if he's all right, but of course he isn't, and what a stupid thing to ask, anyway.

Finally, he looks up at me. His eyes are red and a little blood-shot, and his voice is a little unsteady when he speaks.

"It was a stupid thing you did, Alex."

I blink, real slow. I have no idea what he's talking about. Didn't he want me to kill that monster? Or is he talking about letting Erik in? I mean, he did help us, and I guess, if the other vampires were able to get in too, Lupino must have invited someone inside. I search my mind, trying not to look too stupid, and his eyes get a flicker of annoyance that looks so much better than the haunted look they've had all night.

"You should not have offered your life for mine. I am an old man, who has lived quite sufficiently. You are young, you have your whole life ahead of you."

"Oh."

The word leaves my mouth before I can stop it, and as usual, I want to punch myself for looking like a dumbass, again. I only have a few seconds to follow-up, I know, so I search my mind for some way to explain how important he is, how much better my life is because he's there, and how insignificant I really am. I take too long, of course. There just aren't words. He speaks before I have time to formulate a single thought.

"I do not ever want you to do such a foolish thing again. Do you understand me?"

I do, in a way. I would be so pissed at Jimmy if he did that for me, but it's not the same. I'd also understand his reasons. Maybe I can explain it to him.

"Mister Lupino..."

He raises a hand to stop me. He looks angry, not just annoyed, but really pissed, some kind of black, quiet rage that I've never seen in him before. Still, it looks way better on his face than the expression he had before. He doesn't look so old anymore.

"I do not want to hear it. Dying would be one thing. But this... this... unlife... it is not natural. To think of anyone I care for being..."

His voice falters, and he looks away. I think I can still see the rage in his eyes, but there's a lot of hurt, too. And I understand the feeling. I never liked Jack, but I'd hate to think him not being the master of his own actions, of his own fate. To think it was someone I really cared about, like Jimmy, or Luke, or even Lori... I lean forward to put a hand on his arm, but stop myself before I do. I'm not good with touching, even when it's someone I really like.

"Mister Lupino... I will put an end to it. I swear."

He clears his throat and nods once, quickly. I can't stand his pain anymore, and I can't do anything for him, so I try to think of a way to end the conversation that'll sound good.

"You shouldn't stay here tonight. I'm not positive how this works, but I'll bet once these things have an invite somewhere, they can get back in again. Is there somewhere I can take you? Erik has a car waiting."

He shakes his head, and picks up the phone.

"I will call a taxi. I hope it does not offend you, but I would prefer not to ride in a car with... him. And I wish you would not, either."

"I know. But I have some business to take care of before the night is done."

"Of course."

He forces a smile that's not terribly convincing, and I go.

SEPTEMBER 1ST, 12:27 AM

I have a cigarette outside the door while waiting for Lupino's taxi to come. Erik walks up to me from his car, a neutral expression on his face. For a second, I think he's going to ask me how Lupino is, or worse, how I am, and I prepare to bite his head off, but, as I'm starting to get is his general disposition, he's pretty discreet. He extends a hand in pretty much the same gesture Jimmy has to ask for a cigarette. No wonder these two get along. I take out my cigarette case, and it reminds me of Lori. I wonder how she's doing; I hope Luke had a chance to check in on her. I turn a suspicious eye on Erik when I hand him the smoke.

"I didn't think vampires smoked. Don't you guys like, not breathe?"

He shrugs, putting the cigarette between his lips, searching his pockets.

"Don't need to. But it comes in handy when you want to talk. Don't need to eat, or drink, either, but hell, I'm gonna live forever, I might as well have a good time. Anyway, it's not like it'll kill me. You got a light?"

I don't, of course, but I only have to think about the look on Lupino's face to make a flame in my hand for him. He raises his eyebrows and leans down to light his cigarette on it, then gives me a wry grin as he exhales the smoke.

"Bit of a show-off, aren't you?"

"And you're not?"

"Fair enough."

I finish mine, and walk to the edge of the driveway to throw it out; I don't like leaving my butts on Lupino's lawn. Erik watches me. He seems to be waiting. I light another one as I walk back up to him.

"So here's how it's gonna work. We wait for Lupino's cab to get here, we follow it from a distance to make sure it gets to where it's going, and then we head to Fellini's to kill all those bastards. Got it?"

I leave no room for discussion, but I guess either he's not that impressed with me or he's not as good at reading people as I thought he was.

"Not a good idea. These guys are strong, even for you and me, and there are too many of them. We'd better head there after sunrise, like we planned. But we can still make sure your boss is ok. Besides, you look like hell. When's the last time you slept?"

"It's none of your business. I'm fine."

"You look deader than I do, and trust me, I've been dead long enough to know that can't be good for you. After we make sure your boss is ok, we'll head over to my place, and you'll get some rest, and when the sun comes up I'll call your friend Jimmy and we'll head on to Fellini's. All right?"

Great. Like what I need is some dead bloodsucker playing nursemaid with me. I glare at him, but he seems unimpressed, and just waits for my response. He does have a point, though; it takes a lot of energy to get and stay pissed off enough to put up a good fight, and I don't think I've really slept since the house burned down, so I nod, but not because I want to.

"Fine. Let's go to your house. But if I don't wake up on time, you better wake me up."

He smiles, and there's something condescending in his face, but I'm done arguing for the night. I just don't have the energy.

"I will."

SEPTEMBER 1ST, 9:43 AM

I wake up from a particularly unpleasant dream in which Lori is the head of the vampires and is eating her baby, and I'm on my feet before I recognize Erik's living room. It looks like it's still night, but I remember that his windows are painted black, though I feel like I haven't slept for more than half an hour. Erik pokes his head in from the kitchen, and looks at me with a grin. I'm about to snap at him for making fun of me, then I realize I'm standing in his living room in my underwear, 'cause I have only one suit left and I didn't want it to get mussed. I settle for sitting down and getting dressed in Jimmy's suit, which was still at Erik's place, for the upcoming battle. There's no way I'm getting my only suit dirty, and Jimmy won't mind a little blood on his. Erik is still standing there with his stupid grin, and when I try ignoring him harder, he talks to me, like he can't take a hint.

"Good morning."

"What time is it?"

"A quarter to ten. Sleep well?"

"Hmpf."

I grunt because I don't want to let him know that I didn't, and besides, he should have woken me up earlier than that.

"You were supposed to wake me up when the sun got up."

He shrugs.

"They're not going to be mobile in the daytime, so we have all the time we need, and you needed the rest. I already called your friend Jimmy, though, he's on his way."

I look up at him, shocked.

"Jimmy gave you his phone number?"

"Yeah. How else was I supposed to reach him?"

His question is obviously rhetorical, and he gets back in the kitchen before I answer it. I didn't think anyone else had Jimmy's number, except for me. He doesn't work for anyone but me, and the only way I had to reach him when I first met him was to hang out at his usual haunts and hope he was in the mood for talking. I wonder what it is about Erik that he likes so much. Maybe it's how alike they are; I guess Jimmy's kind of a heartless cold-blooded creature, too.

I hear a kettle whistling by the time I'm dressed, and the sweet smell of brewing caffeine hits my nostrils as I get in Erik's kitchen. He's setting up two mugs, and taking out the bottle of whiskey he shared with Jimmy yesterday, which is now significantly emptier than it was when I first saw it. He's getting a pizza box out of his fridge, and I can see there's not much more in there, except for beer. He lifts the lid and takes a sniff, then puts it on the counter in front of me.

"This is leftover from what Luke ordered for the kids. I think it's still good, but I can't be sure. I don't know how long things really last anymore. I don't eat much, and things seem to go bad by the time I blink."

I look at it. It was only a day ago, and there's nothing growing on it, so it looks good to me. I mean, I've eaten things that had live worms in it before, so if it looks good, I'm sure it is. I shrug, and pull out a slice to eat it cold. He pours the coffee in one of the mugs and hands it over to me, and I put down the pizza to drink it, almost in one gulp. The heat doesn't really affect me; it hasn't since I discovered what I can do. I put the cup down, pushing it towards him so he pours me another one. He lifts his eyebrows and does, but refrains from commenting. I swear, sometimes this guy knows exactly when to keep quiet, though it's unfortunately pretty inconsistent.

There's a knock at the door, and it opens right away. Jimmy's voice calls in to announce himself, which is a courtesy he's never shown me; of course, he likes to avoid coming in to my house, and usually just honks at me from outside. I guess he really does like this guy. Erik smiles at him in a way I find entirely too familiar, and pours him a cup of coffee with whiskey in it.

"Hello, Jimmy."

"Hey, Erik. Alex."

I nod at him. He looks a bit more beat up than he did when he dropped me off yesterday, so I guess he must have had a hard time with Jack, or the thing that used to be Jack, anyway. I don't know how he does it. I mean, crazy is one thing, but if I'd been taken by surprise like that by one of these monsters, I don't know what I could have done without my fire. Jimmy grins at Erik and grabs the cup of coffee, downing half of it in one gulp even though it's still steaming, then he turns his grin on me. He looks to be in a real good mood.

"So, Alex. You ready to go kick some vampire ass?"

I nod. There's a twinkle in his eyes that's only there when he's about to do some violence, like that's all he lives for. He finishes his coffee in another gulp, and I'm not halfway through mine, so I try to catch up. No way I'm going in there without caffeine. I drink up while Jimmy pushes his empty cup towards Erik.

"Can you try to Irish it up a bit more, this time? I fight best with a little booze in me."

Erik shrugs and just fills the cup with whiskey before dropping a little coffee in it. Jimmy grins and nods, picking it up and draining half of it again.

"That's what I'm talking about. Now, come on, Alex, finish getting dressed so we can go burn these assholes!"

SEPTEMBER 1ST, 10:56 AM

The easy part is, apparently, that Erik had an access to the sewers built in his home. I've been in pretty gross places in my life, hell, I've slept in more than my share of garbage heaps, but the sewers beat all of that by a long shot. I'm just grateful there are ledges around the underground river of shit, so I don't have to wade knee-deep in it, even if it is Jimmy's suit I'm wearing. Still, the smell is indescribable, and it's making me gag all the way, though I try not to show it 'cause Jimmy's not saying anything and I don't wanna look like a pussy. Erik's obviously not breathing, the lucky bastard.

After an hour of walking, I can't do it anymore, and I finally ask.

"Are we there yet?"

Jimmy turns a mocking grin on me. I knew it.

"What? Afraid of the smell, boss?"

"Shut up. I ain't afraid, just I'm gonna puke is all."

I hear Erik take a breath, and he makes a face.

"We're almost there. Stop bickering or they might hear you."

"We're that close?"

He shrugs.

"Vampires have pretty good hearing, and we're not far away. Besides, they like to sleep as close as possible to the exit during daylight hours, in case people like us show up from above."

I nod once. It's fair enough. Anyway, as long as we're almost out of here, I'm happy. I feel like the smell's becoming part of me. We finally reach a ladder made of bars in the wall, and Erik starts climbing it, quiet like a cat. He disappears into a shaft, and I climb after him, cutting in front of Jimmy. After all, he's the one who said he could deal with the smell.

I've only made it halfway up when I'm stuck under Erik, who's apparently not moving. I shine my flashlight up towards him, but he hisses and waves it away, so I lower it and remain in the dark as to what the hell he's doing up there until he turns towards me, whispering.

"They'll hear as soon as I undo the latch, if any of them are awake. I suggest you climb up here and get ready to go first and unleash a little fire."

I nod, and as he shifts on the side to make room for me, I climb to squeeze next to him, doing my best to work up a good anger. He watches me until he seems satisfied I'm ready, and reaches up to undo the latch. It makes a loud clanking sound, and he pushes the heavy cast iron gate open before backing out of the way quickly. I climb up as fast as I can, and hoist myself up into a dark room.

It looks to be a storage room of some kind. The floor is concrete. It's really dark, and at first I can't see a thing. Doesn't matter, though. Fire's bright enough.

I can feel the movement all around the room more than I can see it by the time I make the wall of fire. The fuckers are awake, then. Good. The wall of fire's weird, and uneven, 'cause I don't have that much control. But it more or less surrounds me, and I can make it expand as I push out my rage towards them. They came after my kids. They came after Lupino. They're gonna die today.

Erik and Jimmy are well out of the sewer shaft by the time the beasts start screaming. I can see them, now, on the other side of the fire. Some of them are burning, a few are fleeing, but you can see that most of them are just glaring at me, or looking at the fire, searching for a weakness in the wall, for a way to get through. Fat chance. I don't listen to their screams, or their pleas. It'd undermine my fury.

Erik and Jimmy are standing as close as they can to me, watching my back I guess, but probably more repelled by the heat than anything else. Then, Erik sees something I don't, and jumps through the wall of fire to get to it. I do see him do it, though, and I can't believe how fast or how far he goes, way up over the fire. I notice Jimmy try, too, but he just has to back away 'cause there's no way he can match that.

A drop rolls down my face. I'm starting to sweat. This can't be good; I never sweat. I can't feel the heat, I think it's part of my powers, so this must be the strain. It's hard to sustain the anger for that long, without an immediate 'cause or target in front of me. Jimmy finally goes off, running, jumping through the fire, and I have just the time to think, if he's able to do that I must be losing it, before something tackles me to the floor.

I can't breathe for a few seconds, but I've had the wind knocked out of me before so I know the feeling and I don't panic, and I take this moment to look at my attacker. His face is all fucked up, with his eyes all white and his teeth super sharp, but I recognize him. It's the boss's son. Perfect. Just the one I was looking for. Before I have time to even think about fire, he yanks me up and throws me. I hit the wall full force with my back, upside down, which knocks air out of my lungs I didn't think I had time to breathe in, and slide to the floor, on my head, in the fire. My head is spinning, and for a few seconds I don't know which way is up, but I'm surrounded by fire and I have to get up. I drag myself up on my knees. I fell behind a bunch of boxes that are now burning. That's good news, and bad, good because the fire's found something to consume besides my rage, so I don't have to maintain it, bad because now that it has, there's smoke to contend with, too, and I'm not immune to that like I am to the heat.

My lungs finally start working again, and I'm already coughing because of the smoke they're filling with. I notice my jacket is burning, which is not helping, so I rip it off. I'll buy Jimmy a new one. I try to get to my feet, though my head is still throbbing and I'm dizzy as hell, when the bastard just tackles me again. This time, I see him coming at the last moment, and I try to brace for the impact, so I still retain the ability to breathe when he pins me to the wall. I expect him to rip my throat out with these too-sharp teeth, and I cringe, but he's just sneering at me, disdainfully, even.

I try to take the opportunity to make some fire, but as I try to summon my anger, a wave of nausea hits me, and it's all I can do not to throw up. I must have banged my head harder than I thought. I probably look out of it, too, 'cause he just snorts at me, and bangs me against the wall again. I can't stop my head from flying back and hitting the wall, in the same damn spot I fell on. This time, though, I see sparks and black spots when I do, no matter how much I try to blink them away. I can still see how disgusted the thing that used to be Lupino's son is with me, though, and I can't say I blame him.

"Pathetic," he says, in his thick accent that reminds me so much of what Lupino's voice must have sounded like, when he was younger. "The man my father used to be would have never chosen such a feeble creature to replace me with. He is even more worthless than I thought he was."

I frown. His words help me focus, which I'm sure is not their desired effect. I see him more clearly, the monster that used to be the son of Domenic Lupino. The thing that obviously doesn't know how impossibly lucky he was in life.

"He's not worthless."

My voice is a little cracked, and I probably shouldn't be making conversation under the circumstances anyway, but I can't help it. I have to know. He throws his head back and laughs, probably at me.

"Oh, is he not?"

He grins and brings his ugly face up right next to mine, so close that our noses are touching, and I can feel how cold he is. I grit my teeth and glare at him. I should burn him right now, hell knows I hate him enough by now, but I have to know. After all, I know how fathers can be.

"You really did come here to hurt him, didn't you? Like some kind of sick revenge? Why? What did he do to you?"

His grin vanishes, replaced by a sneer, and he hisses. I can see the hatred in his eyes, and I think I must have looked the same the last time I mentioned the man my mother made me with. The one I will never call father, no matter what.

"He is pitiful. Rotten. I do not understand how you cannot feel shame to be associated with the likes of him. Do you not see how weak he is? How sentimental, and soft?"

I narrow my eyes. I understand now. This is personal, just like Erik said. I remember the love in Lupino's face when he told me who the people in the picture were. The loss. The man who called himself my father would have never been capable of an expression like that, even sober. I spit out the question, because I still have to ask it.

"He never did anything to you, did he?"

His eyes narrow even further, and he throws me to the side with a roar of rage. I fall in a pile of burning wooden crates, but this time, I'm too mad to be stunned, or even disoriented. I understand, now. Lupino didn't do anything wrong. It's the love this monster can't stand. It's humanity.

I get right up to face him again, ignoring the nausea and dizziness, the smoke and the flames surrounding me, and the blood that's spilling into my right eye from my forehead. I guess the impact with the crates must have reopened one or more of the cuts on my face. He's advancing on me slowly now, licking his lips, obviously savoring his anticipated kill. He thinks he's beaten me. He's in for a surprise. Nothing could have roused the fire in me like his contempt for the man I love most in the world. The man he was lucky enough to call father.

I start the heat inside his chest. He pauses, then grabs at his heart, his face contorted in pain. Good. I want this to hurt. I could make the fire consume him in a fraction of a second, but I don't want to. The anger that fills me right now will only be sated by his suffering. I build it up, nice and slow. Too slow. He still has the strength to take a step towards me. I walk to meet him, spreading the fire inside his body, and by the time I've reached him, he's on his knees, and his expression is pleading when he raises his face towards me.

"Don't... I can make you great. You could be like me, immortal, untouchable!"

I can feel my nose wrinkle with my disgust. There is nothing in the world that could tempt me to make that choice, not even remotely. I lean my face closer to him, and it's my turn to hiss through gritted teeth.

"The only thing I want from you is to hear you scream."

He snarls at me, but I don't give him the time to utter a single word of defiance. I spread the fire far enough for him to feel it in his bones, in his entire being, and by the time his skin is sizzling and cracking, just before he blows up in a cloud of ash and embers, I get my scream. I stand there for what feels like forever, staring at the pile of ash gathering at my feet, unable to tear my eyes away, until the nausea is definitely back, and I'm so disoriented I'm not sure where I am anymore.

A hand closes on my shoulder, and I whirl around, ready to attack. I recognize Jimmy just in time, by his scar. He dodges my elbow, blinks, and then grins.

"S'just me, boss. You good?"

"Jimmy. Yeah. I'm good."

I take a look around. The fire's spreading. The place is so full of smoke I can hardly see anything at all, and I can only wonder where Erik is, and if we've beaten the monsters. Jimmy grabs my arm and starts to pull me, I don't know where.

"C'mon, boss, we gotta get out of here. The whole place's gonna burn down."

I follow him, stumbling a bit. Why am I so dizzy? I can hardly think.

"Did we win?"

"We're good. Nothing to worry about."

He's coddling me. Why is he coddling me? I must look pretty bad.

"Don't humor me. Tell me the truth."

"Ok. When we're out of here. I can't see with all this smoke, so I'm not gonna sit down and have tea and biscuits and a long good talk with you."

I want to protest, but I'm not sure what to say, so I let him lead me through the smoke and fire. I think he's going to take me up the stairs, but before I know where we're going, he's disappearing down the hole that leads to the sewers again. I turn to look for another way out, but my murky brain somehow summons the logic to realize that it would probably not be a great idea for a couple of people with ties to organized crime to be seen walking out of a building that's just been set on fire, so I follow him down.

The sting of the smoke is immediately replaced by the acrid stench of the sewers. Was it that bad when we were walking through it before, or did it get worse because of the smoke I've been breathing? I can see that Jimmy and Erik are waiting for me at the bottom, chatting in a low voice. I slip on one of the rungs of the metal ladder, and come crashing down into the muck below. Jimmy pulls me to my feet immediately, an expression of disgust on his features as he looks me up and down.

"Man, don't ever ask me to loan you a suit again."

"Sorry."

"S'all right."

I lean against the fence, my head still spinning. The nausea isn't going away, but if I haven't puked yet, standing ankle-deep in shit, I can't be that badly concussed. Jimmy, on the other hand, seems like he ought to be. He looks like his face was smashed into a pile of bricks. There are little cuts everywhere, and the skin on all the right side of his face is red, already turning purple. He's going to look lumpy and swollen in a few hours. I wonder if it'll improve his looks. It is on the side of the scar, after all. There's concern in his eyes when he watches me, though. I don't like it, especially coming from him.

"You ok, boss?"

"I'm fine. Banged my head a bit. Looks like you got worse."

He shrugs.

"I'll live. Let's go, this place stinks even worse than I remember."

Erik nods and starts off in the direction we originally came from, and I follow him, grateful that I wasn't the one to say how bad the smell is.

"So, did we get them all? I was a bit preoccupied with the... with Nicola."

Erik gives me a look, but I can't read his expression.

"We got'em all. All that were there, anyway."

I frown. That doesn't sound like a victory.

"What do you mean, all that were there? You think there are more?"

He shakes his head, and his certainty relieves me a bit.

"I think most of them were there. All the ones who were really into making trouble, anyway. And we got the ones who were in charge. The rest, if there's any, won't be coming back for more."

"How can you be sure?"

Erik grins at me, and I'm a bit disconcerted by his sudden look of pride.

"Hey, give me some credit. I've single-handedly been keeping any and all other vampires out of my city for half a century, now."

I look at his face carefully, trying to see if there's a lie in his eyes, or a hidden motive. I can't find one, which doesn't mean that it's not there, of course. But I think I should be able to trust this guy by now.

"All right. If you're sure. And..." I turn to Jimmy on that one. I never liked the guy, but I still have to know, if only for Lupino. "...what about Jack?"

Jimmy nods.

"He was there. Now he's ashes."

"Right. Thanks."

Maybe I should have had Jimmy gather up his ashes or something. For Lupino. Doesn't seem right to just leave him there, to scatter with what'll be left of the building, and the ashes of the other monsters. I didn't like the guy, but I guess I respected him. Come to think of it, maybe I should have picked up something of Lupino's son. Not like a souvenir, exactly... damn, I'm not good at this family and loss stuff. Jimmy pulls me out of my thoughts.

"So, what's the plan now, boss?"

I look up at him for a few seconds, and I remember that I'm supposed to be in charge. I look back down at the sewer sludge we're trudging in.

"Go back to Erik's place. Wash up. Change. And then... I gotta get back to the motel."

SEPTEMBER 1ST, 6:42 PM

The sun is setting by the time Jimmy drops me off at the motel. I know I look like crap, and I will try to avoid seeing the kids until I'm better, but I have to see at least Luke to tell him it's over. That the kids are safe. And maybe I should see Lori, too. Make sure she's staying as clean as Luke promised he'd keep her.

I inspect the courtyard and the pool as Jimmy's car idles. At least, Luke kept good on that promise, 'cause all the kids seem to be safe indoors. It'll be good to tell him that there is at least something in the world they don't need to worry about.

"Boss? You want me to drive you somewhere else?"

Jimmy's voice pulls me out of my thoughts, and I noticed he's turned off the engine. I must have been thinking longer than I realized.

"No, no, I'm fine here. Thanks."

He nods, and watches me, waiting. The left side of his face is purple and swollen, and with the scar, he looks grotesque, like an old-timey circus freak. I wonder how I look. I haven't really looked at myself since I tried to shave after the shower. I had to give up, of course, 'cause there's too many cuts on my face. Not that I'm that beardy anyway, but the random patches of hair look ridiculous. Probably, no one would notice under the rest of the mess.

I try to think of something to say to thank him, make him understand how invaluable he is to me, but there aren't any words. Besides, I know this is his idea of a day well spent. So I don't say anything as I open the door and step out of the car, but before I close it, he leans towards me. Is that concern on his face? That's twice today. Before now, I wouldn't have been sure he was capable of the emotion, but I guess anything could happen. Two weeks ago, I didn't believe in vampires, either.

"I'll be drunk, but you can call me anyway if you need me tonight."

"Sure. Thanks, Jimmy."

He nods, probably not capable of any more human emotions, and I shut the door. He starts the engine again, driving slowly away while I make my way to the stairs that lead to the second floor, where all the kids' rooms are. Where Lori's room is. I stop at the bottom, and light up a cigarette to give me time to think. What am I gonna say to her? I inhale the last puff before I've found even the ghost of an answer. So when I climb the stairs, it's Luke's door I knock on first. There's a bit of shuffling on the other side, and in a couple seconds, he's opening it, frowning at me.

"You look like hell."

"Thanks."

He stands aside, inviting me in without saying the words, just like I told him to. I smile and walk in, and he seems a bit relieved that I can. The TV's on in the room, and I see that Lori's asleep on the bed, so I stand in the entrance right next to the door so I don't wake her. I watch her for a few seconds. She's pretty, when she's asleep. She almost loses the junkie thinness, the circles under her eyes, the track marks on her arms. I dig up the cigarette holder and pull out a smoke, and Luke folds his arms, looking at me over the rim of his glasses.

"Don't even think about it. If you want to smoke, you can go back outside."

I consider this for a second.

"Come with me?"

He sighs, but smiles.

"Sure."

We step outside and he closes the door behind us, leaving it open just a crack, I guess so he can hear if Lori wakes up or not. I lean on the railing and look down at the pool, and he takes the same position, looking at me, quietly. I guess he's letting me talk first.

"So, we shouldn't need to worry about the vampires anymore."

Luke nods, as if he expected this.

"Figured as much, what with your face being smashed in again and everything."

He can always make me smile, no matter what the situation. I look over my shoulder, but the door isn't open wide enough for me to see through. Still, I can almost see her, on the bed, inside.

"How is she?"

Luke keeps his face carefully neutral as he shrugs, so I know it's gotta be pretty bad.

"Better. I didn't find anything on her, and I've been watching her. She's been clean. Since you left."

I nod. There's at least a minute or two of perfect silence before I confess.

"I don't know what to do, Luke. She can't have a baby on drugs. Not my baby. But I can't make her do anything she doesn't want. What should I do?"

He sighs and leans his head in his hands, looking down over the rail.

"I don't know what to tell you, Alex. I had a talk with her. She says she wants the baby. I think she thinks it'll make you love her."

What can I say to that? I know nothing of love. I don't think anyone's ever loved me. I'm not even sure she really does, or can, through the haze of all the drugs she takes. There must be a reason that I hate to see her high so much. She's not Lori when she's high.

"I don't know if I love her, Luke. But I know I care about her. And the baby... if I'm going to bring someone into the world, I want it done right. You know?"

He nods, not saying anything. I know he knows. He's like me. Damaged. Could any one of us be a good parent?

We're quiet for a while. I have time to finish my cigarette, and light another one, almost smoke it all the way before he speaks again, pushing the glasses up on his nose, like he does when he's real nervous.

"I know a good rehab clinic. You could probably afford it, too."

I frown at him.

"Rehab? You think it'll help?"

He shrugs. He doesn't seem too convinced.

"I think she can't do it alone."

"Fair enough."

It seems to be the end of the discussion. We stand in silence for two more cigarettes, and then Luke stretches and smiles at me.

"So, what do I do with the kids now that the monsters are gone?"

It hadn't even entered my mind. He's so good at taking care of them, I don't really think that much about it.

"How's it going at the house? You know, with the insurance?"

"Repairs should be done in a week or two. We'll be ready to move back in a couple of days."

"Good, good. Sounds like you've got everything worked out, as usual."

"Can you afford to keep us here that long, though?"

The look on his face makes me smile. He doesn't know me that well, after all.

"Of course. The emergency money should be more than enough to cover for this, and I'm making some more, don't you worry. Starting tomorrow, I'm back in business, no more monsters to fight, only goons to shake down. And they're a lot easier than undead bloodsuckers, that's for sure."

He looks relieved, and I have to smile. He should know that apart from the cigarettes and suits, I have practically no expenses, save the ones I make for the kids, and that's really not as much as you would think. The other guys, they all have drug habits, huge houses and expensive wives to sustain. Not me. So I have money, instead, and no taste for it. I flick the butt of my last cigarette over the rail, and turn to him.

"You'll be all right here?"

He nods.

"Got everything under control. Are you going somewhere?"

"Gonna get my own room. After all this, I think I need to sleep for a week."

SEPTEMBER 12TH, 9:45 AM

I catch my knee shaking again and I stop it. I pull out my cell phone and take a look at the time again. Only fifteen minutes left. I was hoping she'd see me today, but I guess I'm out of luck. The nurse at the counter lifts her eyes above her glasses, reminding me of Luke, but that's the only thing that does. Her face sags with wrinkles that have never known a smile. She looks annoyed, but I think that's just her natural disposition.

"Yes?"

"You sure you told her that I was here?"

She rolls her eyes.

"Personally. If she's not here, then she doesn't want to see you. Like yesterday. And the day before."

I turn back to sit on one of the chairs in a row in the waiting room, but I can't. I'm too pissed off. It's been over a week since I brought Lori to the rehab clinic, and signed her in myself. She agreed to go, after a long discussion, but since I dropped her off I've been to visitors' hour every day, asking to see her, and every day, she's failed to come out of her room. I'm not sure what I did to deserve this. I did bring her here, but she knew being clean was a condition for keeping the baby and being with me, and she chose this.

I can't sit back down, so I pace for the next fifteen minutes, until the visitors' hour is good and over. Then I walk out, finally lighting a cigarette. Jimmy is waiting for me in the parking lot, as always, sleeping in his car, which is a Volkswagen today. I get in, and he wakes up, blinks at me twice, clears his throat and starts the car. He takes another, more careful look at my face before putting it in drive.

"She didn't come today either, huh?"

"No."

I scowl at the dashboard and light another smoke, handing him one. I take another look at what he's wearing. The black suit I bought him just four days ago is already crumpled, looks slept in, the shirt is unbuttoned at the collar and he's not wearing a tie. I click my tongue at him.

"And that's what you're wearing?"

"It's just a funeral. It's black, isn't that what counts?"

I shake my head as he lights his smoke and hands me back the silver case. I close my eyes and try to get rid of my sudden headache. We're at the cemetery long before it's gone.

Lupino's there, shaking hands with a few others of his Capos, guys I've brushed shoulders with but no more. I walk in, but stand back, partly because I don't really belong among them, partly because Jimmy's hangover embarrasses me. Lupino notices me and nods in my direction, he starts waving me over, but the priest takes his position and calls everyone to gather, so I step quietly to the back of the very small crowd while Jimmy stays back near the entrance. The priest begins to speak in a droning voice, in Italian, in front of the two small graves. There was nothing left of Jack or Nicola to bury, or nothing we could be sure was them, at least, so there wasn't any need for coffins, but I think Mister Lupino gathered some personal effects or something because there are two small urns waiting to be put in the ground. The priest carries on in words I don't understand, makes a few gestures, calls for a few rites at which everyone seems to know what to do except Jimmy and me. I try to look appropriately somber and am silently grateful that no one is paying any attention to me.

The ceremony lasts almost an hour, after which everyone goes to the pile of dirt in the middle of the graves, takes a handful of it, and throws it on each of the graves. I fall in at the back of the line and do as they do, then stay out of the way as Lupino says his good-byes. I've never been to a funeral before, so I'm really not sure what to say when the others walk off and he comes to join me. He puts a hand on my shoulder and gives me a wan smile.

"Alex. Thank you for coming."

"Of course, Mister Lupino. I wouldn't dream of missing it."

He nods, takes another look towards the graves, and back to me.

"How are things? Are you settled in, yet?"

"Well, I didn't have a lot of things to move, so it's been pretty easy. The condo is nice, though."

There's no need to tell him how empty and lonely it's been since I got my own place. He'll just insist I move in with him again, but I can't do it. I have enough worries without putting the ones I care about in danger just by living with them. He just nods. Does he look sad?

"That is good. And how is your girl... Lori, is it?"

That makes me truly uncomfortable. He knows Lori's pregnant, because that's what I used as an excuse not to move in with him, but I don't know if he knows she's in rehab. I don't know what he would think of her, of me, if he did. I wonder if he found out, in that weird way he has of knowing everything. He gives me no indication either way, so I just nod.

"She's good."

His smile gets a little warmer. I guess he must not know after all.

"Glad to hear it. You will bring her for dinner soon, yes?"

"I'll... try. She hasn't been feeling well."

He nods as if he understands.

"It can be difficult. I will ask Rosanna if she knows any tricks that could help her feel better."

"Thank you."

He looks at the graves again, especially the one marked for his son. He sighs, and it seems like he has trouble looking at me in the eye for a little while.

"Alex, my boy... I owe you a great debt of gratitude."

I'm not sure I understand, so I let him go on, take his time. He takes a deep breath, never looking at me, staring at some point in space above the graves.

"I never knew... what happened to my son. I suspected... but... his body was never found. All these years..."

He sighs, and then smiles at me.

"You gave me the ability to rest. Grieve. Move on."

I must look blank, which is how I feel, because he shakes his head.

"I am sure that someday, you will understand."

I nod a bit. I want to say something comforting, or at least intelligent, but I'm not sure I know what. I was never good at that kind of stuff. So I say the only thing that comes to mind.

"I would have done anything, Mister Lupino."

He looks up at me again with an odd expression, kinda sad, but a little happy, and proud, at the same time. I think. He raises a hand to pat my upper arm.

"Come. Let us go see what Rosanna has made us for lunch, shall we?"

OCTOBER 5TH, 6:47 PM

I take another sip of my coffee and check the time on my cell phone. The jackass is late. Again. I had my doubts when I put him in charge, and every chance I get, I see that I should have listened to my first instincts, even if I didn't really have anyone better to do the job. I've had enough, this time, though. I don't put down the phone, but dial Jimmy's number. It takes him a couple rings to answer, and I tell him to come pick me up. If Chris hasn't shown up by the time Jimmy gets here, I'm coming down to his place and kicking the crap out of him. I'm not sure I won't do that anyway, to tell the truth. I blow out the smoke and put out my cigarette in the aluminum ashtray before signaling the waitress for more coffee. The little old lady sitting at the table across from me gives me a dirty look, piles some change on the table and gets up to walk away. Good. She was bothering me anyway. They're talking about passing a law in this town against smoking even outside. Fucking hell. I know I smoke a lot, but I ain't gonna fill up the entire atmosphere with my smoke, and if anyone could, one city's smoke ban isn't gonna do dick to stop it.

My coffee's just arrived when Chris shows up. The bastard doesn't even have the decency to look ashamed of himself. He's grinning, and his step has kind of a swagger in it, like he's proud. He turns the chair around to lean his arms on the back as he sits in front of me. I pull up my sleeve and look at my wrist in an exaggerated gesture, even though I'm not wearing a watch, to let him know how I feel about his tardiness. He doesn't seem to notice, just grins at me.

"Hey boss!"

I sigh, and take a sip of my coffee.

"You're late."

He rolls his eyes, still smiling, and waves his hand dismissively.

"It's only like, twenty minutes or so."

I take out another smoke and make fire between my fingers, holding it there for a moment before I light my cigarette with it, then stay quiet and glare at him for a few moments. He doesn't seem to take the hint. I guess when everyone in your organization already knows you have superpowers, it's not that impressive anymore. I vanish the fire and breathe out the smoke.

"It's half an hour. And I don't appreciate being kept waiting. I've mentioned this already."

He shrugs, and starts to look inside his coat. I'm so pissed, it's hard to contain the fire; the coffee in the mug I'm holding starts to boil. Again, he doesn't notice, and I take a closer look. His eyes are half-lidded, and his pupils are huge. His movements are sluggish and uncoordinated, and his eyes are bloodshot. I try not to hiss, but I talk through my teeth.

"Are you high?"

He shrugs one shoulder, looking halfway between amused and guilty, but the kind of guilt you have when you're caught eating cookies before dinner.

"So what if I am?"

I breathe through my nose. The fire's been hard to keep down, lately, and with this issue being so close to home, it's hard not to burn him alive right now. But he's just an idiot, and it's not his fault. Well. Not totally, anyway, though I'm sure the drugs didn't help.

"You know the rules. You do not get high before coming to see me. I shouldn't have to be telling you this."

He raises his hands, showing me the palms.

"Hey, relax, man! You can be such a tight-ass!"

I throw away the smoke, reach over and grab him by the shirt, twisting the cloth and pulling him down, my hand right under his chin, so that the collar is wrapped tight around his throat. He gasps, and his eyes go wide. I put my face close to his, close enough to smell the weed on him. I keep my voice low. I don't want to make a scene, here, and it's not the volume that counts, but the tone. Besides, from his expression, I can see I'm making the right impression on him.

"You listen close, asshole. We are not friends, you and me. I could never be friends with the likes of you. You have a job to do, and you report to me, that's all there is to it. If you don't take that seriously, if you don't show the proper respect, or if you show up late or high one more time, you and me are gonna have a problem. Got it?"

He nods, and I let go of his shirt. I pick up my coffee and blow on it, deliberately. He's breathing hard, and I can tell that he's wondering what to do.

"Now hand over the money and get out of here. You make me sick."

He grabs the envelope out of his jacket, dumps it on the table and scrambles away. Some people give us glances, but I don't care. This place isn't one of my usual, so all I have to do is not come back. I pick up the envelope and take a look inside. I'm not sure exactly, but there seems to be less money than there should be. I don't have the leisure to count it right now, so I try taking a sip of my coffee, but it's too hot. It doesn't burn; I'm pretty much immune to all sorts of heat, but it doesn't taste like much when it's this hot.

I take out a cigarette and sigh, rubbing my face in my left hand. It's been a long day. It's about time it was over. I see movement at the corner of my eye, and I turn, expecting Jimmy, but it's some weird-looking guy I've never seen before, wearing a hundred-buck cheap ready-made suit, sunglasses and with his hair slicked out on the side with way too much gel. He stops at my table and smiles at me. I take a sip from my coffee, trying to ignore him. He doesn't go away, though, and even has the affront to flip the chair that Chris was sitting on so he can have a seat at my table. I look pointedly at the dozen or so empty tables on the terrace, and then back at him, eyebrow raised. It doesn't faze him. What is it with people testing my limits, today? Did I wake up in Testosterone City?

"Can I help you?"

"Alex Winters?"

I frown, and take a closer look. This guy doesn't look like a cop, or a lawyer, or even a wise guy. What could he possibly want with me?

"What do you want?"

He reaches inside his jacket, and I scramble to make my thoughts ready to burn him alive before he shoots me, but he only pulls out a business card. I take it. Who knows? Whatever it is he has to say might be interesting. It's printed with blue raised ink, and has a weird medical-like logo on the right. The left side simply says GenEx Group and has a phone number under that.

"I'll take that as a yes. My name is Donald Finley, and I represent GenEx Facilities. Have you heard of us?"

"Never."

I put the card down and resume drinking my coffee, trying to look as uninterested as I can, which is actually hard because I'm kind of curious now.

"We are a corporation that works with people of your... particular abilities."

I raise an eyebrow. That could mean many things, when it comes to me. But when people are this vague about it, it usually means my ability to manipulate fire with my mind. He's got my attention now. I've never met anyone else that could do the things I can. Maybe this guy has. Then again, maybe not.

"So?"

"So, as you may suspect, people like you are few and far between. Our purpose is to help them."

The only way this guy has heard of me is through what I do; he should know better than most how well I've done for myself in the past few years.

"I don't need any help."

The waitress starts to come this way, but I wave her away. I don't want others overhearing this conversation.

"Fair enough. However, we could help each other."

I light another cigarette, this time using my lighter. There's no need to show off now, and I'm starting to think maybe I should put a lid on it, if people like that are seeking me out in cafés I don't usually go to.

"Keep talking."

"Our facilities are dedicated to try and understand what makes you so... unique, but also how such miracles can be physically possible."

Try and understand? That doesn't sound like anything I want to have any part of.

"That sounds like research."

"Well, yes, part of our raison d'être is research."

"No way. I'm not anybody's guinea pig."

"You misunderstand me. Through our research, you would have better control of your abilities. You would be able to accomplish things you never even thought to try before. None of our experiments are harmful, or even unpleasant. And in return for your help, we could provide you with opportunities better suited to your... talent."

I take a moment to consider him, watching him carefully. He looks like a snake. There is no way I'm trusting this guy, he's got the stink of dishonesty all over him.

"I've got plenty of opportunities right here. If you heard of what I do, you heard I'm good at it."

"I'm sure you are. But this would require far less of your time, and we could pay you handsomely."

"I'm already paid handsomely. I'm not interested."

"We could beat any price you throw at us."

I frown at him. He has to know I'm a man of means; and judging by how cheap his suit is, he probably isn't. The fact that he's willing to pay anything arouses my suspicion. He's way too desperate; this has a catch so big I'm surprised I don't really see it.

"I said I'm not interested. Now get out of here."

"Is there nothing I can say to change your mind?"

"Do I need to spell it out for you? Aren't you science types good with words? Not. Interested. Now scram."

He shakes his head slightly, sighing, but stands up.

"I'm very sorry we couldn't come to an agreement. Have a good day. Until we meet again, Mister Winters."

I finish my cigarette, watching him go, making sure he's walking away, and I get another one out of my case, bringing it to my lips. Just as I'm about to light it, I see Jimmy coming to join me on the terrace, and I get my wallet to leave a twenty dollar bill on the table instead of lighting the smoke, getting up. He joins me, and looks like he was about to settle down, but when he sees me leave, he just shrugs and follows. I hand him a cigarette, 'cause I know he was about to bum one, and I light up as we walk toward the car. I'm about to walk around to the passenger's side, but he throws me the keys, and I have to think fast to catch them. I try not to groan. I'm not in the mood for his driving lessons today.

"Again?"

He shrugs, taking out his Zippo to light his smoke, going toward the passenger's side.

"Yeah, again. How you gonna learn if you don't ever do it?"

I sigh. He's right, and I did promise him I'd learn this year so he doesn't have to drive me around all the time. But I'm in a foul mood, and I know what that does to my skills.

"Fine. But it's your funeral."

He chuckles, letting out the smoke and sitting down in the car.

"Seeing as I should have had ten funerals already, I'm pretty confident."

"Whatever."

I start the car, and I stall the engine before I've even pulled into the street. I swear at it, and Jimmy laughs at me. I breathe through my nose as I start the engine again.

"Shut up, Jimmy. Why can't you get a nice automatic, anyway?"

"I do it all for you. If you don't learn standard, it's not worth learning how to drive at all."

"I don't care. I'm never gonna buy a standard car!"

He shrugs, and stays quiet as I pull into the street. I have to concentrate on everything I do. I've only been learning for a couple weeks, and so far, I hate it with a passion.

"So, how'd things go with Chris?"

"What? Oh. Usual, I guess. There's something I don't like about that guy."

"Yeah, he's kind of a dick."

"There's something more, though. He showed up high today. And I didn't have time to count to make sure, but I think his payment wasn't all there."

"What did you do?"

"Well, I put him in his place about the drugs. But I couldn't look in the envelope until he was gone."

He stays quiet for a minute.

"So... I'm guessing you want me to look into it?"

"Yeah. Would you?"

"Sure."

I slow down for another stop sign, and even though I don't come to a complete stop, I still manage to stall the car. I curse at it, start it up again, and Jimmy laughs at me. It's a while before he starts talking again.

"So, I ran into Joe Tyler today."

I slow down for another stop, and don't come to a full stop before I go through. I'm going a little fast, but at least I don't stall this time. I'll pay the ticket if I get one, I don't care, as long as I don't have to start in first gear again.

"So?"

"So, he tells me you gave him another week for his payment."

I grit my teeth, and I press on the brake too hard at the red light, stalling the stupid car again. The key clicks in the ignition three times before I realize I'm not pressing down on the clutch.

"So what? It's my decision."

"Well, you can't just do that. That guy's been late for three weeks, now. You've gotta do something about it. Set an example."

"Why don't you do it yourself? It is kind of your job."

"Well I can't very well do my job when my boss keeps giving him extensions, can I?"

I press too hard on the gas pedal, and the car jumps forward. I try to calm down. Whatever I think about paying tickets, it's not like I actually want to get pulled over. Jimmy should know better than to talk business with me when I'm driving.

"Look, I tried. He had his little girl with him. She's only five. What was I gonna do? It's not her fault! She shouldn't have to pay for what her dad did wrong!"

As soon as the words are out of my mouth, I regret saying them. This driving shit is taking way too much of my concentration; I can't think clearly anymore. Jimmy's face darkens, and he scowls at the road, his expression so violent I wonder if he's not going to jump me, no matter what he feels about me. His dad sold him to a brothel to settle a gambling debt when he was seven years old, but that never stopped him from idolizing the man. I don't get it, but Jimmy's real sensitive about it, and he's already made it clear that he resents any implication to the fact that his old man was anything less than awesome.

"I'm sorry, man. I didn't mean anything by it."

"Just drive."

I keep driving for a couple more blocks, but the tense silence and the stupid standard transmission are getting to me, and by the time I'm halfway to my house, I'm really, really pissed off, and gritting my teeth so hard I probably grind off all the enamel. Jimmy sighs, and rolls down his window.

"Just calm the fuck down, already, Alex. It's getting way too hot in here."

I take a deep breath, and try to clear my thoughts. I don't know if it's because I use it all the time, but I've gotten pretty strong lately with this heat thing, and I have to be careful when I get pissed off, because I make the air around me real hot, and since I don't feel temperature change, I don't notice. It must get cooler, though, 'cause Jimmy doesn't comment again, and he probably thinks it's funny, like he usually does, 'cause he doesn't look so pissed off anymore. He grabs my pack of smokes from the inside of my jacket, while I have my hands on the wheel and can do nothing to stop him, and lights another one. He does it to annoy me; he knows I'm not good enough to do anything else than drive, at the moment, and he usually doesn't smoke in front of me when I can't. He takes a couple of drags, and then clears his throat, picking the subject up like we were never interrupted.

"Anyway, the point is, you're way too soft. I know you don't like it, but everything has its limits, and you can't just keep protecting the hookers and letting guys who owe you money get off easy anymore. The guys are starting to talk, and I'm having trouble keeping a lid on it."

I frown, and nearly miss the stop sign. After starting the engine again, I glance at Jimmy. He's not looking at me, watching the road.

"What do you mean?"

"Come on, man. This is costing money. You can't do what we do and be nice to everyone."

"Lupino's nice."

"To you, sure. He likes you. And I'll admit, he's old school, when mafia meant something more than drugs and hookers. But he didn't make all that money and rise to where he is by bending over for everyone."

I take time to consider it. I don't like to think about it, but I know what he means. I guess by the time I met him, he was well established, and everyone doing the dirty jobs was way below him in ranks.

"What do you want me to do?"

"I told you. Be firm. Don't let things slide. No matter what. If you keep up what you're doing right now, none of the guys will take you seriously anymore. A lot of them are already disrespecting you, some even in front of me, and I can't keep covering for you anymore."

I sigh. When I took over from the Borodinski group, it was to protect the kids that had inadvertently fallen under my wing. At first, that's all there was to it, protecting them. Then, I needed to make money, and to defend my territory against groups that would have taken it over for their own. Now that I'm part of Lupino's group, and things have been running smooth for a couple years, I can't pretend I'm just surviving anymore. This is what I do. I have to do it right, or I'm not going to be able to hold it together.

"Fine. Don't worry. I got it."

He nods. He knows I take this seriously, or he wouldn't still be working for me. We don't say anything more until we reach my place.

ACKNOWLEDGEMENTS

No book ever comes to life in a vacuum. There are people without whom this story might not have ever been written, and there are people without whom I would have never written a word at all... or I would have given up decades ago. To all those people, words seem like these awkward little scribbles that could never hope to be anything more than inadequate to express my gratitude, but, as is often the case, they are better than silence.

To Mathieu, my partner in all things, thank you for being the place I go to when I need to work myself out of a mess I've made with my plots, and for not leaving me when I get into those moods that dry writing spells leave me in.

To Phil, thank you for being critical, for making me double-check everything, for making me ask questions, all of which have made me go so much further, so much faster than I thought I'd ever be able to, and for being there when I need advice.

To my wonderful mom, Danielle, thank you for encouraging me to pursue my dreams, for teaching me that the only thing that truly matters in life is following your passion, and for reading this one and helping me put down the demon of self-censorship.

To Jessica, Johanne, Manon, Marie-Claude, Marjolaine, Caroline, Franck, Manue, Felix, and Annie, thank you for having read it first, for helping me fine-tune it when I was too close to see the problem, and for helping me keep going when I was discouraged, whether you knew you were doing it or not.

To Mister Fein, my father Yvan, and my aunt Loulou, thank you for fostering my love of writing, be it by offering me awesome notebooks, or making me talk about my problems by writing short stories. You taught me not only that writing was a worthwhile endeavor, but that it could be an amazing balm on the soul, as well.

Finally, to the talented team at Renaissance Press, thank you for bringing this to life, and for pouring your hearts and souls into projects like these.

ABOUT THE AUTHOR

Caroline Fréchette is a sequential artist and author. She has published several short stories, both sequential and traditional, as well as two graphic novels, all on the French Canadian and European markets. She was the editor and director for the French Canadian literary magazine Histoires à boire debout, and works in a library. She has been teaching creative writing since 2005, and manages the writing page Ice Cream for Zombies. This is her first novel.

www.ingramcontent.com/pod-product-compliance
Lightning Source LLC
Chambersburg PA
CBHW071301250626
47159CB00004B/1263